"YOU'RE A GUNFIGHTER," I SAID. "A SHOOTIST. ME, GAMBLING'S MY GAME, OR TO BE EXACT, POKER, WHICH IS A MORE HARMLESS WAY OF EXPRESSING MAN'S DEEP-ROOTED ANTI-SOCIAL DRIVES THAN YOUR BUSINESS IS. WOULDN'T YOU AGREE?"

Hardin's eyes were squinting again, but confusion had replaced deadliness.

"I thought so," I said amiably. "What sort of chance would a card player like me have facing down a shootist like you? What are my odds?"

That's when I drew on him.

Not to shoot him. Just to let him look down the long barrel of my .44, and think about it. And think about whether he ever saw anybody that fast with a gun before ...

ABOUT THE AUTHOR

Max Allan Collins has earned an unprecedented six Private Eye Writers of America "Shamus" nominations for his "Nathan Heller" historical thrillers, winning twice. The lastest Heller novel is *Carnal Hours* (1994). A Mystery Writers of America "Edgar Allan Poe" nominee in both fiction and non-fiction categories, Collins is also film reviewer for *Mystery Scene Magazine*: his recent work includes screenplays, short fiction, graphic novels and the occasional film novelization.

A long-time rock musician, he is currently recording and performing with two bands. He lives in Muscatine, Iowa, with his wife, writer Barbara Collins, and their son, Nathan.

MAVERICK

a novel
by Max Allan Collins

based on a screenplay
by William Goldman

A SIGNET BOOK

SIGNET

Published by the Penguin Group
Penguin Books Ltd, 27 Wrights Lane, London W8 5TZ, England
Penguin Books USA Inc., 375 Hudson Street, New York, New York 10014, USA
Penguin Books Australia Ltd, Ringwood, Victoria, Australia
Penguin Books Canada Ltd, 10 Alcorn Avenue, Toronto, Ontario,
Canada M4V 3B2
Penguin Books (NZ) Ltd, 182–190 Wairau Road, Auckland 10, New Zealand

Penguin Books Ltd, Registered Offices: Harmondsworth, Middlesex, England

Published in Signet 1994
1 3 5 7 9 10 8 6 4 2

Signet Film and TV Tie-in edition first published 1994

Printed in England by Clays Ltd, St Ives plc

In memory of Brother Bart,
Jack Kelly
(1927–1992)

"You can fool some of the people all of the time,
and all of the people some of the time . . .
and those are very good odds."

—Beauregard Maverick, a.k.a. "Pappy"

1

Necktie Party

How such a once-fine tree had managed to take root in this desolate landscape was anybody's guess.

It sure wasn't the spot you'd choose for a picnic with your best gal. Dried clumps of grass clung to the sandy earth like the last desperate wisps of a balding man's hair; here and there, prickly pear cacti and cholla stood yearning for some blame fool to brush up against them. Not much chance of that, with all this Godforsaken space to stretch out in.

Poor choice of words, I guess, coming from a man attending a hanging.

Three men on horseback were casually gathered

about the hanging tree, its gnarled limbs reaching their claws into a darkening sky. Thunder growling in the distance, and a gathering, whipping wind, spoke of a storm coming. A bad one.

The tall dark stranger sat there atop the roan gelding, his hands tied behind him, a thick rope tied tight around his neck, the rope thrown over one of the witch-finger branches above. This was plainly not his lucky day. About the best he could hope for was to die before the storm hit.

He was a broad-shouldered, handsome devil in a wide-brimmed black Stetson, frilly white shirt, and Levi's—respectable clothing that had been dirtied and mussed in the recent beating he had been administered. He'd often displayed a sunny, good-natured smile, which had seen him well through his thirty or so years, although right now that smile was understandably absent. At the moment, his well-chiseled face was puffy and dirty, blemished by bruises and abrasions.

Even so, I'm not doing this handsome devil justice. Try to imagine the kind of dashing, heroic-looking type every woman would swoon for—the sort of man's man just about everybody instantly liked.

Everybody, that is, except the three men on horseback who had invited him to a hanging.

Three of a kind is usually a pretty good hand in the game I play, but then, I'd never run into face cards this ugly before. Each one of these raw-boned, stubble-pussed, leather-skinned jaspers was more hideous than the next, from the buzzard whose eyes looked in various directions, to the varmint whose own scruffy neck bore the horrible burned-in scar of a noose from a previous, presumably less-successful hanging.

Then there was the leader, a glowering, black-bearded bandit in a wide-brimmed black sombrero and a weather-beaten cavalry jacket stripped of its epaulets and ribbons. His nickname was somebody's idea of irony (not mine): the Angel. Or maybe they called him that because his shoulders were as wide as a seraph's wing-span. At any rate, he was huge and dirty and dusty and meaner than a sackful of snakes.

Thunder rolled in the hills, and the three outlaws had to rein their horses to prevent a miniature stampede; the horse under the handsome devil about to be hanged had better manners. Whether deaf or well-behaved, the gelding kept his position.

I had trained Ollie well.

You may be wondering why the handsome devil about to be hanged was sitting on *my* horse. The answer is ridiculously simple: *I* was that handsome devil.

You may also be wondering why I took this long to 'fess up to that fact. Since we're going to be spending some time together, you best learn one thing about me right now: I don't show my hole card till the betting's done.

Maverick is the name, of the Texas Mavericks. There are those who would call me a gambler, and they would be wrong: I make my living playing poker, a game my pappy once described as "civilized bushwackin'." The burly, bad-tempered Angel—who had tied a rope to my neck, and a tree—was one of my more recent victims.

He apparently had it in his thick misshapen skull

that I'd cheated him. And cheating is one thing I never do. I don't have to. You see, my mission in life is to exploit my fellow man's ignorance of the laws of probability.

But Angel did not seem to grasp the subtleties of my art.

"Almost got hung once myself, Maverick," the Angel said, his voice about as pleasant as that howling, dust-kicking wind he was straining to be heard over.

I didn't say anything. I didn't want to make any sound or movement that might lurch Ollie out of his well-behaved stupor.

"Didn't much care for it," Angel said. "How 'bout you, Eli?"

His friend with the rope-burn scar shook his head no; he didn't seem to like the idea of hangings at all.

Except, of course, for mine.

"You shouldn'ta oughta made a jackass outa me, Maverick," Angel said.

I was tempted to break my silence and point out that God had beaten me to that one, but—hard as it may be to believe—sometimes I do know when to keep my mouth shut.

"You still wouldn'ta made it to St. Louie for that big game," he said, steadying his horse as the sky grumbled, "but at least you woulda had a future."

My ole pappy once said, "Life is like poker—the outcome's in your hands." But this time I was facing one damn crooked dealer, and my hands were tied behind me.

"We're gonna take our leave now, young Mr. Maverick," the Angel said good-naturedly, "but I don't want you to think poorly of us, after we go."

I just looked at him; I didn't think I had to speak for him to gather my opinion.

Angel said, "Head out, boys," and his hideous companions nodded and left Angel and me behind. They took off in a rumble of hoofbeats that beat the desert floor like a war drum foretelling the storm that was coming.

But Ollie, bless his castrated little soul, stayed still under me.

Angel leaned on his saddlehorn; he was in a ruminative mood. "Y'see, Maverick, I don't think it's a good thing for a man to be alone out in these desolate spaces. Storm comes up, and sky gets to howlin', and your mind can play cruel tricks on you. Starts conjurin' up on ya. Why, a fella can go plumb loco."

He was reaching in his saddlebag.

"A fella needs a friend out in the West, don't you think?"

And he withdrew a burlap bag, about the size of a potato sack.

As casual as a Sunday afternoon game of horseshoes, he tossed the bag toward me, and it landed with a *plop* near Ollie's front hooves.

What was *that* all about?

"Enjoy the compn'y, Maverick."

And then he grinned, displaying the sort of yellow, decaying dentition that had no doubt encouraged Doc Holliday to exchange dentistry for cards, dug his spurs into his mare, and galloped off, raising dust, shaking the earth with hoofbeats.

I craned my neck, much as I dared, to watch Angel's dust-cloud departure. He rode across the flat barren landscape to the rise of a hillock, at the crest of which his grotesque companions awaited. He joined them, and then they were gone, over the hill.

Me, I was feeling a little over-the-hill myself. I had taken a hell of a beating, and I wasn't in the best of positions. On the other hand, I was alone, with the exception of the most imperturbable horse in the West. If Angel thought the coming storm would spook Ollie, or that tossing a burlap sack at the horse's feet would send him rearing, he was woefully mistaken.

All I had to do was wriggle free from this knotted rope around my neck. I took a deep breath and tested it, to see just how taut it was pulled. . . .

Ollie took a half-step.

I hadn't startled him, but my movement had reminded him of my presence, and he must have thought I was considering going somewhere.

"Easy, boy. Whoa . . ."

My soothing tones settled the gelding down, and he resumed his drooping, near-stuporlike position.

A clap of thunder shook the world, and if I'd been a horse, I would have been up on my hind legs and whinnying wildly. The skeletal branches of the hanging tree shook like a symphony of cups rattling dice; even after the thunderclap the tree seemed to be shivering.

Me, too.

But Ollie? Apparently he'd slept through worse storms than this, many a time. He didn't budge an inch.

"Easy, boy," I told him, and kept soothing him as I moved my neck like I was wearing an uncomfortable necktie, and I guess I was—neckties don't get much more uncomfortable than this.

Maybe if I could get my chin under, I could slide the damn thing up and over my face and head. Ollie was keeping still; I had a chance. My sunny smile blossomed, and I breathed a sigh of relief, then almost choked on it.

That burlap sack.

The "company" that Angel had left me, to keep me from going desert daffy.

It was writhing like a belly dancer.

Remember when I mentioned Angel was mean as a sackful of snakes? Here's how I knew whereof I spoke.

That burlap bag seemed to be alive; it moved, it shifted, it traced its awful signature in the dust. But the bag itself wasn't alive; something in it was.

The potato sack was filled with living, squirming things wriggling against their confines, like me working my neck against the rope, only wriggling wasn't all they were doing.

They were also rattling.

Ollie—God love him—didn't notice. This entire affair, thus far at least, impressed him not a whit. He seemed glad for the respite from the hard riding we'd been doing. Though we'd been together a relatively short time, Ollie and me, we were *muy sympatico*.

But the contents of the burlap bag hadn't taken the thunderclap as calmly as my gelding. They had gotten all riled up. And once they found their way out of that sack, and Ollie's sleepy eyes focused on them, and that snout of his sniffed 'em, all our instinctive harmony, and Ollie's natural unflappability, would be gone with the wind.

And there was plenty of wind, right now.

Time to throw caution to it. I worked my chin under the noose, the prickly hemp first tickling, then scraping, and it was tight, and hurt like hell, but what choice did I have? Doing this made me squirm in my saddle, like those snakes squirming in that sack, but Ollie stayed calm. Nothing seemed to fluster him.

"Good boy," I was whispering, "good boy. You're earnin' yourself a great big mess of oats—"

Thunder shook the sky again, and everything under it, except Ollie. He could have been a statue of a horse. Clouds were rushing like an angry posse across the sky, searching out any patch of sunlight and blotting it out, creating a charcoal-colored eclipse illuminated by only the occasional streak of lightning. The jagged bolts were veins of silver in the cavern of the sky.

The noose was up to my nose, just under it, as I peeked over the rope at the sack of snakes.

And it *was* a sack of snakes: I knew that for sure, now. Angel, though he wasn't present, had showed me his first card.

A rattlesnake peeking out of the bag.

"Jesus," I said softly.

It was partly a prayer. Partly it wasn't.

Fortunately, Ollie hadn't noticed the diamondback as it slithered from the sack. But how long he could remain oblivious, I couldn't hazard a guess.

Not when half a dozen more rattlers were now gliding out of the sack, making lazy S's in the dust, so very near Ollie's hooves. Funny how many different sizes of rattler the Good Lord, in his Infinite Wisdom, had decided to put on this Wicked Earth. Oozing from the mouth of that sack were all sizes of serpent, ranging from big to enormous.

They weren't angry yet, in fact, they seemed to be pleased about their freedom. After all, they were smiling.

Fangs like these would've given Doc Holliday pause, too.

Me, I just kept my own wriggling going, trying to work my nose under and the rope up, praying that Ollie stayed complacent or asleep or whatever it was that was keeping him from snorting and shying at the sight of the rattlesnake cotillion holding forth at his feet.

Tell you the truth, I was shaking with fear, and if that strikes you as cowardly, friend, that's your problem. As my old pappy used to say, "A coward dies a thousand deaths, a brave man only one. A thousand to one—that's good odds."

But I'd been bucking the odds all week. And sometimes even a percentage player like yours truly can use a smile from Lady Luck.

2

A Friendly Game

Somebody stole my horse out of the stable in Elwood, Kansas,—some sore loser, probably—and there wasn't much I could do about it. Marshal Dooley and I weren't exactly friends, and I'd created too many suspects at the poker table in the Weeping Willow Saloon to bother with any investigating of my own.

So I'd bid a less-than-fond farewell to that saddle-burr of a city, and headed for greener pastures. With a saddlebag full of cash, I could have afforded something more thoroughbred than the mule I was riding, but I was counting pennies. The poker game of the century was starting in St. Louis in just ten days, and I was still three thousand dollars shy of the entrance fee.

Coming up out of a dusty canyon, my mule clip-clopping along, I encountered a wagon train heading out to the promised land. I nodded to the pioneer men with their dark hats, heavy beards, and somber faces—religious folk, most likely, maybe Mormons—and tipped my hat to the calico-dressed ladies, who smiled shyly and looked away. In the back of one of the wagons, I spotted two boys, ten or eleven, playing cards. Hope for the next generation.

The locals probably thought of Crystal River as a jewel nestled along the bank of the tributary whose name the hamlet had borrowed. In truth, the twin-rutted, hard-packed dirt road led into a main street, layered with river sand to keep dust to a minimum, that revealed a frontier town a mite nastier than most. Sure, you had your livery stable with peaked hayloft and blacksmith forge out front; and there was Trapnell's Mercantile and Hargrove's Hardware side-by-side, sharing a brightly painted wooden awning that shaded a plank porch, and Heyes Apothecary with huge jars of colored liquids and sun-faded pills in the window.

But mostly you had a series of clapboard buildings with elaborate facades that boasted of more saloons and gambling halls than Wichita and Dodge City put together.

In other words, my kind of cow town.

I'd come to Crystal River to take some money from the bank—not to stick it up, of course. In one of life's sweet little reversals, the local banker owed me money, though he had a nasty habit of ducking payment. Just as my mule was jostling its way down Main Street, a stagecoach rolled off the barge-style ferryboat and rumbled down the thoroughfare. River sand or not, some dust got kicked up, much of it in my face.

Not that it mattered; at this point I was covered with more soil than your average back forty.

I reined my mule up in front of the bank, where a sign informed me the Crystal River Bank was closed till tomorrow morning. I groaned, both at the unintentional bad pun and the prospect of losing more time.

If I could just collect a few debts between here and St. Louie, one of which was the local banker's, I'd sew up the entry fee for the All Rivers Poker Championship. No need to look elsewhere for funds. No need to be tempted by the gambling halls of Crystal River.

On the other hand, gambling never tempts me. One of the most commonly held misconceptions about me and my brother Bart, is that we're gamblers. Call us that at your own risk: we're Texans, and easily insulted.

I'll have you know, we are poker players.

And the way our pappy taught us, poker ain't gambling at all.

So when I hitched my mule to the post outside the Crystal Palace—an establishment so grand that it had a second floor and a sign advertising ROOMS—I wasn't capitulating to temptation; I was heeding the voice of inner reason. I found my way to the desk, and the balding clerk, with his pinched-nose glasses, pinched up his face as well at the sight of what was presumably just another no-account, dust-covered trailhand.

"May I help you, sir?"

I reached in my shirt pocket and withdrew a single, folded, square of currency, and I unfolded it and revealed it in all its hundred-dollar-bill glory.

"A room," I said, tossing the bill at him. "And a hot bath."

"Yes, *sir!*"

His smile and change of heart were so sudden and radical, I just had to grin. Shaking my head, I signed the register, gathered my change, then—saddlebag over my shoulder, rifle in hand—headed up the stairs.

"Oh, sir!"

I glanced back; he was reading my name in the register.

"You have a telegram!"

"Bring it here."

He came over eagerly. "You want me to read it to you?"

"No."

He did anyway: "It just says, 'Watch your back.' There's no signature. Do you know who it's from?"

"Yes."

"Here," he said conspiratorially, handing it to me, and scurried back to his desk.

I glanced at the wire, folded it up, and put it in the pocket where the hundred-dollar bill had been. Then I went upstairs.

And if you're wondering who the telegram was from, don't waste your time waiting for me to tell you.

That's my hole card.

After a hot bath, I felt human again. When I headed down the stairs around dusk, in my black Stetson, black clawhammer coat, string tie, green-and-black silk vest, and the most beautiful ruffled white lace shirt a Paris tailor ever sewed, I must have been a vision.

Certainly the Crystal Palace was—a rustic vision of spinning wheels and rattling dice and greenbacks passing from one hand to another. Doing a pretty good business for this time of day; the bartender was sure keeping busy. Customers ranging from cattlemen to local merchants were trying their luck at roulette and wheel-of-fortune, the hourglass cage of chuck-a-luck lured others, while a good many settled in at tables where faro, red dog, and twenty-one were being dealt.

I was in my element.

But none of those games was my game. The view of this frontier casino, as I came down those stairs, reminded me of the time my pappy gathered up Bart and me, when we were no higher than the buckle on his hand-tooled belt, and walked us into an El Paso saloon. He swept his hand out in all-encompassing gesture, and his voice was as stern and commanding as a revival tent preacher's.

"Boys," he said, "take a long hard look. This is what's known as gamblin'. Stay away from it. In games of chance like these, a man hasn't got a prayer."

I nodded at Bart, and Bart nodded back at me.

Then Pappy smiled and said, "Boys . . . stick to poker."

There was only one poker game going, and nobody worked for the house. That was the way I liked it. The only rule of my pappy's I consistently break is this: "Son, never play with strangers. The fellers you know are trouble enough."

But a man who plays poker as well as I do has to move around to get action, and a man who travels as much as I do, even somebody who doesn't like bucking the odds, has to take a few chances. And because of that, I ease into a poker game the way I had eased my big toe into that hot tub of water upstairs. Just testing it.

So before I even inquired about the empty chair, I watched a while. Sized up my fellow players.

Three of them were your typical run-of-the-herd players—win a little, lose a little, content just to break even. One was a cowhand who swore frequently, then would apologize to the man sitting next to him, a preacher, who said, "Thank you, Jesus," when he liked his cards. The other ran the hardware store and bet a little too much, but not enough to matter.

The other three players were more interesting. There was a kid who looked barely old enough to be in the place, a skinny runt in a milk-chocolate derby hat and a dark jacket he swam in. Looked like if he sipped a drink through a straw, he was in danger of falling in.

But the sixgun he wore, in a well-oiled holster tied down to his leg in the shootist manner, said not to take him lightly.

Next to him, wonder of wonders, was a beautiful woman. Well, maybe not beautiful, but right pretty and, to somebody who'd been on the trail-to-who-knows-where in the company of a mule for the last two days, a sight for sore eyes. She wore an elegant satiny gown, midnight-blue, her blond hair tied back in a bow, a black, beaded-glass necklace glittering at the creamy curve of her neck. Her face was made up, but not dancehall-gal heavy.

She didn't play poker very well, but was a real whiz at flirting.

Next to her was one more player, whom they called, for reasons unknown, Angel. Bearded and sullen under his wide-brimmed black sombrero, he was huge, smelly, and nasty-looking; he would've made a buffalo skinner just stepped in off the range look for another seat.

But the lovely lady didn't seem to mind—most poker players, good or bad, wouldn't. They love the game.

Angel sat there scowling at cards dwarfed by the powerful hands he held them with. In a week, he and some pards would be stringing me up to a tree, and tossing a sackful of rattlers my way. But he didn't mention that, and somehow I neglected to ask about it.

"Is this chair taken?" I asked.

"It is now," the gal said. She had a Southern accent as lilting as a songbird's mating call, and as phony as a politician's campaign promise.

I pulled out the chair, gave her a smile, and she gave me one back that was even better.

"My name is Annabelle Bransford."

She offered her hand and I took it.

"Bret Maverick, ma'am," I said. "Of the Texas Mavericks."

She looked me up and down, taking in the string tie and frilly shirt. "You wouldn't be a professional card player, by chance?"

"Not by chance," I said, sitting. "On purpose."

I showed my sunny smile to my fellow players, half-rising to make some quick and informal introductions, accompanied by a shake of the hand, when I gazed into the glaring, bull-like, nostril-flaring countenance of the one called Angel. He was clutching the deck of cards in his big paw, making it look like a box of kitchen matches, and had no intention of shaking hands with the likes of me.

"I like the game the way it is," he growled.

"Now don't go off half-cocked," I said, turning the wattage up on the smile. "I bring all kinds of plusses to the table."

"Such as?"

"I hardly ever bluff and I never, ever cheat."

"I don't believe you."

"Sometimes I have trouble doing that myself. But this time, so happens I'm telling the truth."

"I like the game," Angel said, his voice rising, not in volume, but in intensity, "*just* the way it is."

"Bet I can change your mind." I got out some cash, ruffled the bills. "I plan to lose for at least an hour."

"Game is five-card draw," the Angel said quickly, his eyes wide with my money.

And for an hour I did lose, often to Angel, as did the others—not surprisingly, a bully can often intimidate players into giving him pots he doesn't deserve, scaring 'em out with big bets.

It takes me an hour to get the feel of the game, to figure out who's strong, who bluffs and when, and where the raises'll come from. Once I have the people down, then I can pace myself accordingly.

The kid in the derby had a pretty good poker face, and he always held his cards close to his sunken chest, to keep anybody from seeing. But I saw that every time he had a good hand, he held those cards so tight, he damn near squeezed 'em to death.

Now the cowhand: the better his hand, the more casually he pitched in his chips.

The Angel had a "tell" when he had a borderline hand: he'd do a sort of slow shuffle of his five cards, moving the top card to the bottom, the top to the bottom, over and over.

The preacher, well, he must have said a prayer before every bet, 'cause he stared at his cards for a long time before committing that-which-is-Caesar's to the pot. And when he did bet, he had 'em.

But tonight, the Lord wasn't giving 'em to him often.

The hardware store man fiddled with his tie when he had a good hand, but had to try to figure out whether his hand was good *enough*.

And Annabelle had three "tells" in all, the cutest being when she flicked her thumbnail under her pretty little white front teeth, indicating she was bluffing. She bluffed often and not well, though occasionally she hauled in a big hand, and at times seemed almost as good a card player as she was a flirt.

I soon knew when not to bet against her: whenever she had a dead-sure lock-solid hand, she giggled girlishly and went into an I-declare-a-poor-little-thing-like-me-can't-hardly-tell-heads-nor-tails-of-these-silly-cards singsong.

There were other things to learn from. Like the way they kept their chips: Annabelle kept hers well organized, neatly stacked; the Angel was slovenly, the chips scattered in front of him as if they'd been spilled there; the cattleman couldn't quit fiddling with his, particularly when he was playing out one of those so-so hands the amateurs don't know enough to fold.

After an hour and a half, I hadn't won a hand. I threw in my cards—Angel had won another round—and stood.

Angel grinned. "Had enough?"

"Necessary room. Hold my chair?"

Coming back from the water closet, I stopped at the bar for a drink. As I leaned against the counter, I could see through the windows that darkness was settling a gentle hand on Crystal River; a few citizens were out strolling the boardwalk, a lamplighter was at work, carriages with lighted lanterns glided by.

Back to work.

Annabelle raised a pretty eyebrow at the sight of my glass of water. "You look more like the bourbon-and-branch water type."

I sat and gave her the smile. "My ole pappy said, 'Son, never touch hard liquor or hard work.' Good advice, all 'round."

Angel gave me his nastiest look, and that was pretty darn nasty. "I think I heard just about all I care to about this 'pappy' of yours."

"You don't seem very happy to see me, Angel," I said, "considering I'm the fella who's making you a wealthy man."

That set him to grinning yellowly, and he forgot all about my pappy.

"Let's play poker, then," he said.

"Let's," I said.

A few hands later, I caught three sixes; it was down

to just me and the kid in the derby. He turned up his cards: two pair, aces over queens.

"Well," I said, showing him my sixes, reaching out for the chips piled in the center of the table, a good-sized pot, "maybe luck's my companion, after all."

The kid was touching his left eyebrow, rubbing it; he was squinting, as if his head hurt. He mumbled something I didn't quit catch.

"What was that, kid?"

"I, uh, said . . . I don't think that hand should count."

He sounded like an eight year-old who'd just woken up in the middle of the night.

"You don't think the hand should count." I looked at the other players and they all shrugged; even Angel seemed surprised by this whiny little outburst. "You got any logical sorta reason for that, son?"

He spoke so softly I could barely hear him: "My mind wasn't on the game."

"Your mind wasn't on the game. Okay . . . well, tell you what—"

And I stopped, because he was looking at me now. I didn't know this boy, but I knew the look. I knew the eyes. They were cold and hard and pity was a stranger to them.

They were the eyes of a killer.

"What's your name, son?"

"Johnny Hardin," he said.

Now, he didn't have to be John Wesley Hardin. I'd heard Hardin, believed to be the deadliest gunfighter in the West, preferred "Wes" as a nickname. But I'd also heard Hardin killed his first man at eleven.

"What's your trade?" I asked.

"Guns."

"You sell guns?"

"No."

"I see. Gunsmith, then?"

"No. Mostly, I kill people."

I had to ask these questions; after all, Pappy says, "Never bet into a blind hand."

"Since you're still alive," I said, "I have to figure you're pretty darn good at it."

The eyes narrowed, just a touch. "Care to find out?"

The soft little voice had turned as deadly as the eyes.

I studied him. Both my hands were on the table, still poised to pull in my chips. My fingers rolled on the green felt cloth, drumming easily. Then I grinned.

"Not really," I said. "We'll say this was a practice hand, okay?"

Hardin nodded slowly.

I sat back, gestured toward the pile of chips. "You take whatever you think you got comin' to you. I'll be content with the leavings."

Annabelle, who I think had been taking kind of a shine to me, suddenly was looking at me with abject disappointment. It's a look I've seen on women's faces before.

Angel, on the other hand, wore contempt like a bandit's bandanna, only he wasn't hiding behind it; he was displaying it for the world to see.

"You *always* been this gutless?" he spat.

I thought about it. Then I nodded. "Think so. At least as long as I can remember."

"Gutless," Angel repeated disgustedly, shaking his head.

"My old pappy always said, 'He who fights and runs away lives to run another day.' "

I slid back in the chair, and it made a grating, scraping sound on the wooden floor that got everybody's attention. I stood, drew open my coat, pulling it back so everybody could see the .44 Colt revolver in my own well-oiled leather holster, tied down to my thigh.

"Tell you the truth," I said, "I think being brave is highly overrated. What did it get Custer?"

The kid was watching me, his hand hovering near his gun. Annabelle's look of disappointment was gone, but she now seemed to be wishing she'd picked a more civilized room to do her gambling in. All the other eyes at the table were on me, too, including Angel's, which were narrowed in a singular combination of shrewdness and stupidity.

"You're a gunfighter," I said. "A shootist. Me, gambling's my game, or to be exact, poker, which is a more harmless way of expressing man's deep-rooted anti-social drives than *your* business is. Wouldn't you agree?"

Hardin's eyes were squinting again, but confusion had replaced deadliness.

"I thought so," I said amiably. "What sort of chance would a card player like me have facing down a shootist like you? What are my odds?"

That's when I drew on him.

Not to shoot him. Just to let him look down the long barrel of my .44, and think about it. And think about whether he ever saw anybody that fast with a gun before.

Judging by his stunned expression, I'd say he hadn't.

"Why, I'd have no chance whatsoever," I said casually.

Then I gave my gun the Texas twirl my pappy taught Bart and me and the Colt slid smoothly, snugly, back in its leather home.

Annabelle leaned toward the kid conspiratorially and asked, "Was that fast?"

Hardin swallowed and nodded, once.

"I thought so," she said, and nodded too. "Looked fast to me."

I sat back down and picked up the cards. "My deal, isn't it?"

"Yessir," the kid said.

"Might I make a small suggestion? That henceforth you keep your mind on the game?"

"Yessir," he said.

"Draw!" I said.

Hardin twitched in his chair, but I held up my hands, one of which held the deck. "Draw *poker*. It's my deal, remember?"

Several sighs of relief, a few coughs, and some muttering filled the moment of silence that otherwise was broken only by my shuffling of the cards.

Annabelle smirked and whispered. "That was kind of a dangerous jest, wasn't it, Burt?"

"That's 'Bret,'" I whispered back. "And, no, I don't think so. I think Johnny's off his game, now."

I began the deal, and when I got to Angel, he didn't seem particularly impressed by my little gun-handling demonstration.

"You say you like playin' cards?" he asked gruffly.

"With a passion."

"How come? When you lose all the damn time."

I just smiled and kept dealing. "Oh, I don't lose *all* the time—sometimes I do for the first hour or so."

"What happens after that?"

"Probably I'll win all your money. Jacks or better to open, gentlemen . . . Miss Bransford."

"That's Mrs. Bransford," Annabelle said.

"Pity," I said.

"Check," the hardware man said.

"Check," Angel said. "Aren't you a little overconfident, Maverick?"

"No. Experienced. Check to you, Reverend. Can you open?"

And, of course, I began to win. Not every hand, but most of them. The kid would hold his cards tight and bet, and I'd double it, and he'd fold. The cowman would make his oh-so-casual bet, and I'd double it, and he'd fold. Annabelle would giggle girlishly and bet, and I'd fold, and she'd win, naturally. The Angel would make a big bully of a bet, and I'd make a bigger one, and he'd fold. The hardware man would fiddle with his tie and bet, and I'd raise big, 'cause I knew that even though he probably had some good cards, he didn't have cards this good.

And I'd win.

It went on like that for some time. There were two trends: everybody but Angel was getting cleaned out by yours truly, and everybody but Angel was taking it well.

Angel, on the other hand, frustrated that his big bets weren't driving me out often enough, was getting red in the face with anger. Right now, he had one of those borderline hands, I could tell: he was doing that slow shuffle with his five cards.

And his eyes said it, too: he had a pretty strong hand, but was it strong enough?

Apparently he had figured out his bully-boy tactic wasn't working, so he made a reasonable bet and sat back.

And I made a big bet. Actually, a huge bet—pushing damn near all my chips out into the center of the table.

"Shit!" Angel said, and flung his cards on the table.

"You win," Annabelle said to me.

"Ma'am," I said, and tipped my hat. I put my cards down and started pulling the chips in.

Angel was half out of his chair, reaching across the table, his hands on my discarded cards.

"You didn't pay to see those," I reminded him.

"I paid plenty!" he snarled, and turned my cards up.

I had a King high. Not much of a hand in draw.

He was on his feet, roaring, "You didn't even have a goddamn pair!"

"No I didn't," I said. "Not that it's any of your business."

"You said you never bluffed!"

I raised a gently lecturing forefinger. "I said I never cheated, and I don't. I said I *hardly* ever bluffed. This was one of those 'hardlys.' "

Angel was trembling. It was not a pleasant sight. Maybe the rest of his name was "of Death."

"You cheated the whole goddamn game."

"For an hour and half, you beat me, friend. Fair and square. But I was paying attention, and you weren't. Once I had your 'tells' down, well . . . things just kind of worked out in my favor. That's the way the game is played."

Those enormous hands were squeezing themselves into fists the size of hams.

"I just called you a *cheat*, mister."

I shrugged. "You also called me 'gutless,' a while back. I figure you was just funnin'. It's a friendly game, after all."

Angel was red with rage, blind with fury, his bearlike arms reaching across the table, hands clawing for my coat. I was standing up, knocking my chair over, backing up and away, when I heard the voice behind me.

"That's *him!*" somebody shouted. "That's *Maverick!*"

"There *is* a God!" another harsh voice said. "Stand away from him, pard—you can have the bastard when *we're* done with him!"

3

Showdown on Main Street

The voices were familiar and, when I glanced behind me, so were the unshaven—and furious—faces of the four burly cowhands shouldering their way through the Palace patrons, moving toward me as inexorable as winter. Each of these men was nearly as big as the Angel, if not quite as ugly (though admittedly the odds against finding four men ugly as the Angel are longer than I'd care to go up against).

But collectively, they made the threat of a confrontation with the Angel seem like an invitation to a church social.

They had come bursting through the double-hung

bat-wing doors, and the one in front, a square-jawed, hard-eyed hombre, had his sixgun drawn.

And, friends—when they already have a gun in their hand, it don't mean diddly-damn how fast you are.

Annabelle, much as she may have cared for me, moved out of harm's way, though I could feel her eyes stay on me. The other players rose and backed away from the table, even Angel, although the fearful expressions of my fellow poker players did not extend to him: he was grinning. Eating this up.

Didn't mind at all, sharing me with these interlopers.

I turned slowly toward this four-man lynching party as they advanced ominously toward me, and I held up both hands, palms out, in a calming gesture.

"Let's not do anything rash, gentlemen," I managed.

"When I spotted you through that winder," the hard-eyed hombre said, "it restored my faith in the Lord Jesus."

"Then you best do the Christian thing," I said, backing up against the table. My hands were still up and out—a lot of witnesses could see I had no gun in hand and was making no move to change that fact.

"What, turn the other cheek?" the hombre sneered. "You already gave it to us in our hindquarters, Mr. Mav-ar-ack."

I didn't much care for the pronunciation, but I let it go.

"Boys," I said soothingly, "you shouldn'ta been playin' cards, drinkin' heavy like that. Poor judgment. Poor cards. Whose fault is that?"

The hombre's hard eyes flared. "*Yours*, you thievin' son of a bitch."

And he thumbed back the hammer of the single-action Colt, cocking it, and the tiny click made an enormous sound in the quieted-down room.

You could've heard a card drop.

That was when I vaulted over the card table, upsetting it, cards and chips flying, Annabelle, Angel, and other patrons of the Crystal Palace scattering as I made a path through the place toward the swinging front doors.

I burst through those doors into the cool outdoors, where a full moon helped the lanterns that lighted Main Street make hiding damn near impossible. Glancing back as I ran, I saw my four would-be assailants practically tear the bat-wing doors off their hinges as they scrambled out, pursuing me onto the sand-covered dirt street, their feet raising powder as they pounded after me.

Annabelle and the Angel followed them, finding positions on the porch of the Palace to watch the show.

Is *that* what they wanted? A *show*?

I stopped.

Stopped right there in the middle of the street, with the moonlight bathing me in ivory. The world seemed unreal, suddenly, and I found myself turning and facing the four men who were barreling down the street toward me.

And, seeing me stopped like a statue, they stopped too. In their tracks. Frozen, looking at the one fool who was facing the four of them down.

I heard a woman gasp. Maybe it was Annabelle.

Spectators were swarming the Palace porch. I'd given them a real surprise; the jaw on Angel's ugly puss had dropped open like a trap door, and his eyes were wider than they were stupid. Which is to say, mighty wide.

Easily, gently, so nobody could mistake my action for me going for my sixgun, I untied the leather string that kept the holstered sixgun snug at my side. Then I unbuckled my gunbelt and took it off. Bent at the knees, lowered myself to the sandy street, and placed my .44 in its holster on the bullet-studded belt there, as if I were arranging a window display.

Then I stood.

The hard-eyed hombre still had his sixgun in hand. The hammer was still cocked back. But he had a streetful of witnesses who would see him if he fired at me. In this part of the country, it didn't matter who fired first, or even if you hit your man in the back, as long as the other fella was armed.

On the other hand . . .

Shoot an unarmed man, why, you might as well steal a horse. It's going to get you lynched, pure and simple.

The hombre's three pards knew as much, and they looked at each other in a silent conversation of shrugs and lifted eyebrows and humorless smirks, finally allowing their leader to make the decision.

He did.

The hard-eyed hombre nodded solemnly at me, uncocked his sixgun—a very small click in the night—and eased it into his holster. Then he unbuckled his gun belt and lowered it to the sand; so did his three pals, with their gun belts.

The crowd on the Palace porch was getting an eyeful, out here in the moonlight. Johnny Hardin was watching through narrow eyes, and Annabelle was clutching his arm, pressing against him. Lucky guy.

Me, I just had four pissed-off–looking cowhands walking slowly toward me, like they were the Earps and I was the Clanton.

I could have stood there and took my medicine. But like my ole pappy told me so many times, "It ain't how you play the game, son, it's winnin' that counts."

So I charged into them.

Charged like they were unsuspecting toreadors and I was a bull that didn't like the idea of getting swords stuck in me. They didn't expect me to be so fast, and, frankly, I didn't expect them to be so slow.

I took the hard-eyed hombre down first, raising a big puff of sand and dust, then spun around and sank an elbow into the generous gut of the nearest of these human sequoias. But no tree is too big to go down, and he was no exception, doubling over, knees wobbling, *whump*! More sand and dust flying. . . .

Then I did some flying, right into the next varmint, ducking the vicious blows he was windmilling at me, and slipping inside where a punch to the side of what was apparently the glassiest of glass jaws sent him staggering back, knees giving, followed by another *whump* and another minor dust storm.

Turning away from the dust to grab a breath, I glimpsed the wide-eyed spectators leaning forward at the rail as if watching a horse race they'd put all their money on. Annabelle was leaned out farthest of all, her eyes bright, her smile perhaps just a tiny bit sadistic. She was proud of me.

Even better was Angel—his stunned expression had melted into something new and wonderful: fear.

I almost laughed, but didn't have time; a lumbering bear of a cowpoke was about to hug me. I fell on my back and kicked out with both feet and caught him in the chest, sending him careening back, tripping over his own feet, and falling, hard, increasing the cough-inducing dust cloud.

Maybe that was why I didn't see the hard-eyed hombre, who'd recovered from my first tackle, get up and clutch me from behind. I didn't fight him—I went limp.

He didn't quite know what to do with this human noodle, and was finding himself struggling to hold me up when I all of a sudden stiffened like a board, reached back for him, and tossed him over my shoulder. He might've been a big bale of hay.

When he landed on his back, he made a real big impression on Main Street.

Then I noticed the guy I'd elbowed the air out of had made it back to his feet—unsteadily—but he was up. So I went back to see if he wanted some more.

"Enough!"

It was the hard-eyed hombre. He had gotten to his feet as well, and was dusting himself off.

"You won, Mav-ar-ack . . . fair and square."

"It's Maverick," I said, moving forward, fists tight.

"Maverick," he said, apologetically, head bowed, and his eyes didn't look so hard any more as he gestured to his pards. They backed away, and when I moved toward them again, they ran away, making one last dust cloud.

The eyes of my porch-bound spectators were on my

fleeing opponents, and then moved to me. The faces were smiling, admiring, and, in some cases, apprehensive. Both Angel and Johnny Hardin wore grave expressions that let me know I'd made my point.

Casually, I picked up my gunbelt, dusted off the sand, and buckled it back on. With a sharp look toward Angel and the kid, I tied it down to my leg with the leather strap. Shootist-style.

Give 'em all something to think about.

When I pushed back through the swinging doors into the Crystal Palace, I felt calm and collected, considering. I was breathing a little heavily, yes, and all that rolling around in the dust and sand meant I'd have to finance another hot bath in the morning. Such is the price of fame.

Annabelle had suddenly latched herself onto my arm. Her eyes were huge and fluttery and I noticed, for the first time, that she smelled of lilacs. Above the bodice of her satiny gown, her bosom was rising and falling, and doing a right fine job of it, too.

"That was the most a-*ma*-zin' thing," she said, milking her Southern accent for all it was worth. Which was plenty.

I shrugged. "Sometimes even a percentage player gets lucky."

With Annabelle on my arm, as if we were entering a ballroom and not a frontier casino, I headed back toward the poker table, hoping someone had taken the time to upright it and put things back in order. They had.

But before I got there, I caught my reflection in an

ornately framed mirror, only my reflection wasn't ornate in the least.

It stopped me dead in my tracks, just like I'd stopped those four cowpokes outside. Removing Annabelle's hand from my arm delicately, I moved toward my reflection as slowly and suspiciously as two gunfighters facing each other down in the street.

I did not like what I saw.

My ruffled lace shirt, imported from Paris at no small expense, was dirtier than hell. An awful pattern of brown smudges looked like it had been burned into the frilly fabric. The face that looked back at me in the mirror was tight with blind fury.

I strode toward the poker table, where Angel and the others were waiting.

"All right," I said. "My shirt's soiled. Maybe damaged. What the hell else can go wrong?"

I swung around and pointed my finger like a sixgun at the Angel.

"Weren't *you* sayin' something when those children interrupted us?" I snarled.

"No, no, nothin', really," he said, waving his hands in the air as if surrendering. "Nothin' important . . ."

Annabelle, trying to help (I'm sure), touched a finger to her forehead as if trying hard to think back, saying, "Wasn't it something about him being a 'gutless coward'?"

Angel was sweating; he was smiling, too, a shit-eating variety that was no more pleasant than his nastier smiles, though considerably more amusing.

He said, "Never said such a thing, missy. Gutless cheat, maybe, but I would never call this man a coward"—he looked toward me with a placating expression on his hideous scruffy pan—"and I *was* just funnin' . . ."

I looked at him hard.

And long.

As if I were trying to decide whether to kill him with a gun or just my bare hands.

Then I gave him, gave all of them, the sunny smile, pulled out the chair, and sat down. Reaching for the deck of cards, ruffling it, shuffling it, I said the three most beautiful words in the English language.

"Let's play poker."

4

A Southern Belle

I sat on the edge of the bed in my room at the Crystal Palace, counting my winnings. Nigh on to a thousand dollars; not bad for an evening's work, and just that much closer to that staggering St. Louis entry fee.

There was a hundred-dollar bill in the pile, and I safety-pinned it to the inside of my black jacket. Earlier that day, I'd used the century note previously pinned there to impress that snobby desk clerk downstairs.

I don't consider myself properly dressed unless I have a little something to fall back on, pinned in my coat.

But doing that only made me notice how dirty my

pretty shirt had gotten; I was afraid to take it off, for fear I'd find it was ripped, as well.

Shaking my head in sorrow, I tucked the rest of that cash into my jacket pocket and thought about maybe not waiting till tomorrow morning for that second hot bath. My shirt wasn't the only thing that got soiled in the ruckus.

I was considering that when the knock caught my attention—a gentle knock, as if some genteel person hoped not to disturb me. Of course, I hadn't noticed anybody genteel in Crystal River as yet, so I slipped my sixgun out of its holster and went to the door.

"Who is it?"

"It's Annabelle, Bret. Might I speak to you?"

This was a pleasant surprise. Perhaps I'd made an even bigger, better impression than I'd imagined.

Returning the gun to its holster, I opened the door and there she stood, in all her stunning Southern-belle glory, the slightly low-cut gown revealing a creamy expanse of nicely rounded womanhood.

And once again, that lovely creamy expanse was rising and falling—she was nervous. I could darn near see her heart pounding. At least I was sure trying to.

"I . . . I shouldn't be doing this," she said, and started to leave.

I moved my eyes up to a more gentlemanly level. "Annabelle . . . Mrs. Bransford, wait!"

She stopped; she'd only gone a step or two, so it didn't take her long to retrace them. She came back and looked at me with her big blue eyes all fluttery. "Yes, Bret?"

"You're not doin' anything," I said, "except standing in the hallway. I believe that's still legal in this state."

She lowered her gaze. "But I would prefer more privacy than this hallway, Bret."

"Well, step into my room, then. If that's ag'in the law, I won't be the one reports it."

She hesitated a moment, then—as if she'd made a sudden, irrevocable, incredibly crucial decision—rushed into the room in a flurry of satin and petticoats.

"We can leave the door open, if you like," I said.

She closed the door.

Then she lowered her head, covering her pretty face with slender, graceful fingers. "If only . . ."

"If only what?"

She looked up at me with eyes wide and yearning. "If only I weren't a married woman. . . ."

And she flew into my arms and wrapped hers around me, clutching me desperately, her lips finding mine, locking me into a warm, passionate kiss that promised so much, and delivered some, as well.

Then she pushed me away, as if she had just as suddenly regained her common sense.

"Forgive me," she said, shaking her blond curls in remorse and shame. "But I had to do that."

"No problem."

She gestured with one outstretched hand, the other tucked behind her. "You must understand, Bret. . . . My very being . . . my very soul . . . *cried out* for me to hold you. Demanded I cast convention to the wind—"

"Stop by any old time."

From her dazzling smile and her bright shining eyes, you'd think I had just expressed my undying love. She raised her chin, and spoke in a quavering voice that dripped with honeydew.

"We'll likely never see each other again, Bret . . ."

Funny how she could make a two-syllable word out of my name like that: *Bray-att*.

". . . so it may not be ladylike, but it would be safe to come right out and say it . . . to tell you that you're the most overwhelmin'ly attractive man on the face of this earth."

Who was I to disagree?

"There," she said, lowering her head in shame. "There, I've said it."

She moved closer to me, rested her cheek against mine. "And now I must say . . . goodbye."

It was a far, far better thing than she had ever done before.

She floated toward the door like a vision of Southern beauty and gentility. But she was also clearly a woman of passion. And I am, if nothing else, a healthy young man—in addition, of course, to being overwhelmingly attractive.

How could I let her go?

I reached for her, stopped her, took her hand—gently—and guided her back into my arms. My voice was soft, husky in her delicate shell-like ear: "Annabelle . . ."

She was trembling in my arms. "Yes, Bret?"

I gave her a peck of a kiss on the forehead.

"If you don't give me my money back," I whispered tenderly, "I'll toss your pretty backside in the sheriff's lap."

She shoved me away, and her finely hewn features portrayed both pain and indignation.

"How could you say such a cruel and heartless—"

I snapped my fingers. Held out my open palm.

She studied me, then sighed and shook her head. She knew I wasn't fooling.

"Damn," she said.

From behind her back came a delicate hand filled with the wallet that was itself filled with the cash I'd won from her and Angel and the rest of them at the table. She slapped the wallet in my open hand like she wished she were slapping my face.

"Thanks, Annabelle," I said genially, slipping the cash-brimming wallet back in my pocket.

She stood with arms folded, her expression tight and sneering, her eyes shooting daggers.

"Hey, don't be mad at *me*," I said. "I can't help it if you're as bad a thief as you are a card player."

I figured that might make her madder, but she merely shrugged it off, and her sneer turned smirky. "Actually, I'm a good thief . . . even a pretty fair poker player. It's just that I'm havin' a powerful run of bad luck."

"As my old pappy used to say, 'Poker in the hands of an expert ain't a matter of luck.' "

Her eyes flared. "*You've* never had a streak of bad luck, I suppose?"

"Tell you the truth"—I patted the pocket with the wallet of greenbacks in it—"tonight I kinda broke one, with your help. Where are you from, exactly?"

"Didn't I say? Why my people are from Atlanta—"

"No, Annabelle. I don't want to know where the

phony accent's from. I want to know where *you're* from."

That made her smile—ruefully, but she smiled. "Most gentlemen *like* me as a Southern belle," she said, layering on the syrup even heavier. Then, in a flat midwestern voice, she said, "Okay, so I'm not Southern."

"And there isn't a Mr. Bransford, either."

"Just my late father."

"Figures. I didn't take you for the marrying kind."

She flounced her pretty head. "And I never will be, thank you kindly. So . . . what happens now?"

I shrugged. "What could happen?"

A man in a hotel room with a beautiful woman has a right to consider certain possibilities.

Worry touched her face. "You're not going to turn me in, are you?"

"Of course not."

"Why?"

I gave her half a grin. "Maybe I'm havin' mercy on the sheriff."

She smirked again; pointed a thumb at the door. "So—I can just go?"

I nodded.

"Damn," she said.

"Now what's wrong?"

She was shaking her head; her expression seemed more one of frustration than anything else. "It's just that you . . . you really *irritate* me."

"I do?"

"I should be furious with you. You've insulted me, you've stolen from me—"

"Stole my own money back from you, you mean."

"See! A remark like that simply makes me want to scratch your damn eyes out."

"But you're resisting the urge."

"Yes." And she looked at me curiously, trying to figure it out. "It's just that you're so darn . . . likable."

"Now that is a problem. I'll have to work on it."

"You're *doing* it again! Stop it!" Now she looked at me as if sizing me up for the first time. "There isn't a Mrs. Maverick, either, is there?"

"Just my late mother."

"Not a wife."

"I think I'd remember."

She cupped her chin with a hand, tickling her own cheek with a forefinger; her smile was mischievous. "You know what *I* think? I think if we'd met . . . perhaps under different circumstances . . ."

I took a step forward. "Yes?"

"We'd have utterly *despised* one another."

I had to grin; she'd reeled me in with that one.

"See?" she said, grinning back like a kid who got away with something. "I can be likable, too."

"*And* irritating."

Then she was in my arms, smelling like lilacs and feeling very soft under the smooth satin of her gown.

"Goodbye, Bret," she whispered. Her embrace was fleeting, as was the kiss she gave my cheek, and so was she.

But she did pause for just a moment at the door.

"Goodnight, Mrs. Bransford."

Her smile was as tender as it was momentary; then she was gone.

I watched the door, half-expecting, or anyway hoping, she might reappear. But she didn't. Yet her presence lingered, and it wasn't just the lilac perfume.

"Oh, well," I said, shrugged, sighed, and slipped out of my jacket.

And then I began to laugh.

Because I had just noticed the wallet was missing from my pocket again.

Annabelle had packed in a hurry: a satiny bit of something poked out from the top of her carpetbag as she slipped one shapely limb out the window onto the wooden-slat fire-escape balcony beyond her room. The carpetbag was good-sized, and she had heels on her buttoned-up pointed-toe shoes, so it was clumsy going, and she was grunting and groaning in a decidedly unladylike fashion.

"Could I be of assistance?" I asked.

I was leaning against the rail, enjoying the cool evening and the lovely moon; a few clouds, like streaks of white from an artist's brush, only highlighted the brilliant deep blue of a sky sprinkled with jewel-like stars.

"Lovely evening," I said, and gave her the sunny smile.

Poised there in the window, sitting half-in, half-out, she gave me the sourest of smirks. She dropped the carpetbag and it landed so hard the slats of the fire escape rattled.

"You gotta admit," she said, "I was better the second time."

"Smooth as the handle on a gun," I granted. "Couldn'ta done better myself."

"Now, that *is* a compliment," she said archly, but she liked it.

And I gave her a gentle nudge that sent her back into her room, where she fell in a pretty pile. I stepped inside the window, plucked the big snap purse from her lap, and dug out my wallet, tucking it in my coat pocket.

"So there's hope for me yet," she said, smirking and tossing a self-pitying little shrug. Couldn't blame her, really—she'd just missed out on near to a thousand bucks, for the second time in one evening.

"Yes," I said, helping her up, giving her the purse back. "But I been thinking about you and the sheriff, again. Maybe you two *should* get acquainted."

She put her hands on her hips, and her eyes were clear and wide and blue and threatening. "Maybe I should tear my gown and call for help. Seems to me a strange man in a lady's boudoir has scant bargaining power."

She had a point.

"Tell you what," I said. "Why don't you just do me a favor, and we'll call it square."

I took my jacket off, tossed it on the bed.

"Whoa, horse!" she said. "I don't owe you *that* big a favor!"

"Lady, attractive as the prospect might be, I have no intention of going to bed with you. Suppose I doze off? God knows what parts of me you'd run off with."

"Then, what . . ."

I gestured to the sad fact that was my dirt-smudged shirt. "You're a woman."

"Keen observation on your part," she said, wondering what that had to do with my ruffled shirt.

"Well, you must know how to clean somethin' like this. Obviously, I don't. I'm a man."

"So I noticed." Then she clasped her hands and raised her fluttery eyes, slipping back into the Southern-fried patois: "If I cain't touch him, at least I can hold his silken shirt next to my heavin' bosom . . . and *dream*."

"All right, all right . . . will you do it?"

"Of course. Just knowing you equate me with an old Chinese washerwoman has my heart going pitter-pat."

I was unbuttoning my shirt. "Yeah, right. Now, be *careful* with this."

"I'll be as delicate as if it were your very skin."

"That's what I'm afraid of." I handed it to her, slipped my jacket on. "You want me to go out the window, or . . ."

She cracked open the door. "It's all clear. My reputation is secure. And so is yours."

I was on my way out when she gave me one more Southern shot: "Sleep well, Bert."

"It's Bret, and you know it!"

She shut the door on me.

I stood there for a moment thinking about it. Then my hand flew to my coat pocket and felt the reassuring lump of my wallet. I had my poker winnings, but she'd still wound up with the shirt off my back.

5

Wild Card

The next morning, I strolled down Main Street, my mood as glorious as this sunshiny day. Last night's game had put me that much closer to the poker championship entrance fee, and then, of course, there was Annabelle Bransford.

The acquaintance of such a lovely larcenous lass made for a worthwhile addition to my long list of enemies, friends, and friendly enemies. I figured Mrs. Bransford would show up again, down the trail. It was something to long for, and to dread.

I'd already had a fine steak breakfast at the hotel, bought a ticket for a seat on the noon stage, and traded my mule in for fifteen dollars at the livery. I was rested, freshly bathed, smoothly shaved, and ready to travel. Dressed for it, too, in my black shirt and new Levi's, a wide-brimmed Stetson shading my eyes.

And I only had one stop left to make: the bank, which had been, after all, my reason for coming to the scenic eyesore known as Crystal River.

The Crystal River Bank was a modest storefront operation; a few horses were hitched outside, a few customers at teller windows inside. Nice and quiet. The bank didn't seem to have a guard. A clerk who was perhaps a day older than Methuselah looked over his wire-framed glasses at me when I inquired as to the bank president's whereabouts. He pointed me toward an office at the rear.

I rested my hand gently on the Colt .44 at my side as I approached the pebbled-glass door with the gilt letters, MATTHEW WICKER, PRESIDENT. Taking one final quick look around, I unholstered the Colt and burst into the office.

Wicker was standing just inside the door, examining a ledger book plucked from a nearby shelf. He was a distinguished-looking, middle-aged man with a well-tended mustache and a three-piece suit with cravat and jeweled stickpin. He looked up at me from the ledger with the stunned, frightened eyes of a surprised deer.

I closed the door behind me and kept the sixgun trained on him.

Wicker, swallowing, shut the ledger book, placed it unsteadily back on its shelf, then slowly raised his hands, trembling as he held them high. His voice was high, too, in the manner of the heroine in a meller-drama: "Oh no, please don't hurt me, you terrible villain—have mercy on this frail flower!"

"You're playin' the wrong part," I said. "You're the guy with the mustache doin' the foreclosing around here."

The door cracked open and the elderly clerk stuck his nose in, eyes large behind the wire-framed glasses. He took me in and blurted, "Robbery!"

"No, no," Wicker said dismissively. "It's just Bret Maverick saying hello."

And shut the door on the flustered little man.

Then Wicker grinned and held out his hand. "How the hell are you, you silly son of a bitch?"

I holstered the Colt, and we shook hands warmly. Even gave each other a manly little hug. Matty and me went way back.

"Like my pappy used to say, 'Son, today I feel better than a possum eatin' a yellow jacket.' "

"That good?"

"At least. About 'bout you, Matty?"

His grin faded. He shook his head glumly, went to his desk, and sat behind it. "I feel like the yellow jacket that possum was eating."

I sat on the edge of the desk. "That bad?"

His eyes were sorrowful. "Bret, I know I still owe you that thousand dollars from the game in New Orleans. You were an upright friend, taking my marker."

"My pappy says the only marker a man ought ever take is the one the undertaker gives him."

"I know that. And maybe you should've listened to him. Bret, all I can give you is maybe a hundred dollars." He searched a pocket and came up with one lone century note. He handed it toward me.

I took it. I never felt lousier taking a hundred dollars in my life. Not because I was taking Matty's last hundred, mind you; but because of the nine hundred dollars that wasn't attached to it.

"You know me," he said. "I never welched a debt in my life. After all, if you can't trust your banker, who can you trust?"

I chose not to answer that, sighing as I put the hundred in my pocket.

His voice had a plaintive, almost pitiful tone. "Can you give me till the end of the year?"

"I need it now," I said.

He nodded sadly, sighed. "It's that poker championship in St. Louie, isn't it? I knew it. What's the entry fee, anyway? Twenty-five thousand?"

I nodded.

"That's a small fortune," he said.

Indeed, it was a figure that might impress even a banker.

"I don't suppose you could consider a little honest embezzling," I said.

"Bret, I couldn't do that to my fellow citizens. When I went into the banking business, I went straight—you know that."

"Yeah. If you can't trust your banker . . ."

With another heaving sigh, I slid off the edge of his desk and started toward the pebble-glass door. Matty came around from his desk and walked me there, with a hand on my shoulder.

"Jesus, kid—I'm truly sorry. Didn't you take Porkchop Slim's marker in that same game?"

"Slim died last month."

He made a sympathetic clicking sound in his cheek. "I guess I did hear a rumor to that effect. But I didn't hear what he died of."

"Five aces. His widow said he'd held back a thousand for me, but she used it for the funeral. Gave him a real big send-off. Finest one in the history of Baumgarner County, she said."

"Bret, I heard another rumor about Slim . . ."

"Oh?"

"I heard his wife had him cremated and dumped his ashes in the Rio Bravo."

I slapped my forehead. "Porkchop's widow *conned* me? What's this world comin' to?"

Matty raised both eyebrows, and his eyes were wide and doleful as he shook his head. "I know. It's sad. It's hard to trust anybody these days. How shy of that entry fee are you?"

"Just two grand. I know where another thousand's waitin', so if I could just put together—"

"Can't your brother help you out, or is he heading for St. Louie, too?"

"Bart's sitting this one out, but he's already invested five thousand in his older brother."

Matty scratched his head, thinking. "What about your Irish pal, Big Jim McComb?"

"Tapped out."

"Gentleman Jack?"

"In jail till at least Christmas, and Dandy Jim's trying to raise the entry fee himself, I hear."

"Damn. It's a tough one. If I had any cash to spare, Bret, you'd have it sure as shootin'."

He opened the door for me, and a sixgun—sure as shootin'—was thrust toward us.

"My God," Matty said, "it *is* a robbery!"

And a bank robbery indeed was in progress. Several masked men were training guns on both the tellers and the customers, who had hands reaching for the sky. Or anyway, the ceiling.

The gun-waving outlaw facing us down wore a slouch hat and a bandanna. He started by frisking me; he found the hundred in my pocket that Matty had given me. Then he frisked the bank president himself.

And from one of the banker's pockets—not the one Matty had fished the C-note out of for yours truly—the outlaw withdrew a wad of bills thicker than the Holy Bible.

"If you can't trust your banker," I said to Matty, "who can you trust?"

Matty, his hands up, shrugged and half-smiled. "You can trust me now."

Over by the door to the big safe, where several sticks of dynamite were roped around the handle, an owlhoot was lighting a match and touching it to the fuse.

"Here we go!" he yelled, and ducked for cover.

So did I and, I would imagine, everybody else, although I was much more concerned with Bret Maverick's welfare.

The explosion blew the door off its hinges, shattered every window in the place, and did my eardrums very little good, to boot. The only positive effect was the billowing smoke that provided a screen for any level-headed sort who might have the sense to slip out in the confusion.

Like me.

Well, after all, somebody had to go tell the sheriff . . .

The problem was, as I came sneaking out the front door of the bank, appearing in a puff of smoke like an apparition, I encountered four familiar faces.

The last time I'd seen these faces had been on this very street, last night, in the moonlight.

In the sunlight, the faces looked even more menacing.

"Are you crazy?" I said, as they closed in on me.

"Not hardly," the hard-eyed hombre said.

I moved quickly, almost running, the smoke drifting out from the explosion providing more cover as I ducked into the nearest alley and stepped into the shadows, clinging to the wall of a clapboard building.

But they were right on my heels, and my standing in the shadows didn't keep them from seeing me, and approaching me, and surrounding me.

"I told you," I said, "we're not to be seen together. It'll spoil everything."

"If you leave town before you pay us," the hard-eyed hombre said, "that would *really* spoil everything."

"Would I do that?" I shook my head. "There's no trust left in this world. Anyway, I should dock you for coming in so late. A second more, and that Angel character would have torn my limbs off and beat me to death with 'em."

The lead hombre frowned. "Well, nobody suspected anything, did they?"

"No," I said, "I gotta hand you that much. Everybody bought into it."

For a play mounted at such short notice—namely, when I left the poker table for the necessary room, and rounded up these boys in the outer bar—the production couldn't have gone better.

"Truth is," the hombre said, grinning, "we kinda enjoyed it. Thanks for goin' so easy on us."

The other cowhands grinned and nodded and let out a few horse laughs.

"Well, I didn't see any point makin' you suffer," I said. Damn—those had been my best shots! I was slipping. "Anyway, what did we agree on, five dollars a beating?"

The leader nodded.

When I travel, I move my hundred-dollar bill from inside my clawhammer coat to my shirt lining; I slipped my hand in-between buttons and unpinned the bill.

"Hope you boys have change for a hundred," I said pleasantly.

Unfortunately, they did.

After I dropped by the sheriff's office to tell him about the bank robbery that was probably starting to wind down, I went back to my room at the Crystal Palace, where I found a delivery had been made. On the bed was my lucky silk shirt, freshly laundered and wrapped up in tissue paper, with a note attached saying, "Love, Annabelle."

Now wasn't that sweet. A good girl at heart, that Annabelle.

I pulled my saddlebag out from under the bed, took a

fresh hundred-dollar bill from my stash in its draw-string leather pouch, and pinned the bill inside my shirt. As I did that, however, I noticed the shirt was somewhat rank from the smoke that I'd waded through exiting the bank.

Often, when traveling by stagecoach, you encounter a more refined type of folk, so perhaps it would be more appropriate to wear my nicer duds. Nodding at the thought, I slipped the silk shirt out of its tissue-paper wrapping, and immediately noticed something was awry.

Either I had grown considerably, or Mrs. Annabelle Bransford had shrunk the living hell out of it.

Well, I wore the damn thing, anyway. I could barely squeeze into it, but the other shirt stank of smoke, and I didn't have time to get any of my other things laundered. So I was stuck.

The sun was still shining and the day was every bit as glorious as when I'd gotten up that morning, only my mood was considerably darker. I strode quickly down Main Street with my saddlebag over my shoulder and my rifle in hand, and people wisely cleared out of my way.

At the end of Main Street was the dock of the ferry crossing. The stagecoach with its team of four horses was already up on deck, and so was one of its passengers, waiting to board.

Annabelle Bransford.

She was shading herself with a parasol, looking picture-perfect in a beautifully tailored money-colored traveling costume. How I wished I could shrink it for her.

I went up the gangplank onto the deck of the little bargelike ferryboat and joined Mrs. Bransford near the coach. She didn't do a very good job of hiding her smile when she saw what I looked like in a shirt better suited for a ten-year-old.

"You did this on purpose!" I said, gesturing to my chest, where I was damn near popping buttons, and not because I felt proud of how I looked.

"You bet," she said.

"This is my lucky shirt!"

"Not anymore. May I make a suggestion?"

"What?"

"Next time, do your own laundry." She smiled smugly, twirled her parasol, and turned her back to me.

I took her by the arm and spun her around, held her by the shoulders, and glared into big, long-lashed blue eyes that pretended at boredom.

"My underwear comes from New York," I told her.

"How fascinating."

"So where the hell do you think that shirt was made?"

"Lilliput?"

"Paris, France, lady! They don't sell shirts like this in a dry goods store, you know."

"Not unless it's in the children's department."

She squirmed from my grasp and I grabbed at her and she kicked me hard, in the shin. I was doubled over, howling with pain, when a deep, powerful, very male voice boomed out from behind me.

"Remove your hands from that lovely lady!"

Which was a remarkably stupid thing to say, considering at the time my hands were nowhere near the lovely lady, being wrapped instead around my shin as I hopped around on one foot like a wounded jackrabbit.

When I finally put both feet back on the ground, I got a good look at the individual who'd made such an idiotic remark, but to tell you the truth, he presented an imposing, impressive figure.

Tall, raw-boned, wide-shouldered, lantern-jawed, he gazed at me steadily with piercing, slightly beady brown eyes from under a black bowler. His dark hair touched with gray, he wore a well-trimmed handlebar mustache in the manner of Wyatt Earp and Bat Masterson, and—like those legendary lawmen—was something of a dapper dan, sporting a three-piece pinstripe with a red cravat.

Citified duds or not, he wore his sixgun tied to his leg with a leather shootist-type thong, and carried with him a frontier air that would have made instant grist for the mill of Eastern dime-novel writers like Ned Buntline.

He swept off the bowler and made a half bow to Annabelle. "If this young ruffian should distress you in any manner, I do hope you'll allow me to intercede."

Annabelle twirled her parasol and gave him the fluttery eyes, not to mention the full-course Southern-fried treatment: "Sometimes when you *least* expect it, a hero rides in."

"Well, shucks, ma'am," he said, clearly embarrassed.

I'd be embarrassed, too, if I'd said something like "Aw shucks."

She leaned toward him, and if those eyes had fluttered one iota more, I swear she'd have taken off and flew. "But it's true," she said, "Mister . . . Mister . . . ?"

"Cooper, ma'am. Zane Cooper. But I'd be obliged if you'd just call me 'Coop.' That's what my friends call me, and it suits me just fine."

"Coop," I muttered. That wasn't a name. That was a place where chickens lived.

Now the southern belle was bashful, averting her gaze. "Why, Mr. Cooper . . . Coop. I do believe you're a real gentleman."

And she held out her hand to him, and the old coot kissed it.

Now, I don't mean to be ungracious when I call this unwanted intruder an "old coot," but handsome a figure as he cut, formidable as he looked, he hadn't seen fifty since Grant was president.

Annabelle waved a gloved hand at me by way of dismissive introduction. "This silly-looking creature is named Bert Maverick."

"Bret," I corrected.

Either way, Cooper paid me no heed; didn't offer me a hand to shake, nor I him.

"And I am Annabelle Bransford," she said. "I'll be taking this stage, once it's ready."

The smile under the handlebar mustache was painfully shy. "So, I am pleased to say, am I."

They were gazing at each other like lovesick calves.

"I'm on this stage, too," I pointed out, in case anyone was interested.

Apparently not. This ride was going to be one hell of a lot of fun.

Annabelle was standing very near Cooper, now. Confiding in him, but in a voice meant for me to hear. "I just don't know *what* that ruffian might have done, if I'd've had to make this trip with just the two of us, alone, on that stage."

Well, they were in agreement: I was a ruffian.

"Ma'am," Coop said, "now with me aboard, I trust you can relax and settle back and enjoy the journey." He gazed at her warmly. "You know, it's my feeling that if there weren't any women, we wouldn't none of us be here."

"That's a brilliant observation," I said. "If there weren't any men, we wouldn't be here, either!"

Slowly, Coop turned toward me, and those beady eyes bore down on me like he was sighting a weapon. "Were you mocking me, sir?"

"Would it bother you if I was?"

His nod was also slow. "I can get ruffled. You wouldn't like me to, however."

"No, I don't imagine I would. Let's just say I was agreeing with you in an unusual way."

He looked at me long and hard; so, by God, I looked back at him the same way.

"I can't decide," he said, "whether you're a brave man or a coward."

"Maybe it depends on the situation."

A faint sneer formed under the mustache. Then Coop turned, took Annabelle's carpetbag, and set it up and over the railing on the roof of the coach, then slid it inside the luggage compartment behind the rider's seat.

"Wherever would the world be," Annabelle wondered, "without true gentlemen?"

"Ma'am, you embarrass me," Coop said, and gave her a smile even I could envy.

Feeling a little sick to my stomach, I turned to see a corpse approaching.

Well, not a corpse, exactly, but the sickliest-looking old man I'd ever seen. He made the elderly clerk back at the Crystal River Bank look like a spring chicken. His beat-up clothes and sorry-looking hat made me wonder how he'd managed the fare for a stagecoach ride. But here he came, right up the gangplank on unsteady legs, wobbling toward the stage.

Coop wasn't the only true gentleman in the West. I opened the door for the old boy.

"Are you tetched?" the codger asked, his voice as quavery as he was. "I'm the driver!"

"The driver?"

"Well, what's wrong with that?"

"Are you feeling all right?"

His voice was as indignant as it was tremulous. "Why in tarnation is everybody always askin' me that?"

"Why, I have no idea," I said, and shrugged.

"Well," he said, and held out a quavering hand, "help me up, son, or we'll *never* get a move on."

I hopped up on the driver's seat—which was a good six feet off the ground—and reached down to pull him up. It took a while. It was kind of like hauling up a loose bag of kindling, only the loose bag of kindling was trying to hand itself to you. Finally I guided the old gent to his position on the buckboard.

"Isn't anybody riding shotgun?" I asked him.

"What for? We ain't haulin' anything of value. Just passengers."

I didn't feel like discussing the philosophical implications of that statement, nor did I feel like revealing just how much money I had in that pouch in my saddlebags. Which I was keeping with me at all times, by the way.

The old boy snorted his thanks, and I climbed down to join my fellow passengers, who had already boarded the coach.

The ferry was shoving off.

Glancing up at the frail guardian of our destiny, who was seated on the buckboard with the reins in hand, I could hear my old pappy's voice ringing in my ears: "Son, if I ever hear tell of you playin' a game with wild cards, I'll whup you within an inch of your life."

And this game was full of them.

6

Stagecoach Shuffle

The jostle of the stagecoach springs on the already springy deck of the ferryboat could create a singular sort of sea sickness if you let it. I kept my eyes closed as I concentrated on the Maverick shuffle, a one-handed variety my pappy taught Bart and me; first my right hand, then my left. It calmed my stomach and soothed my soul.

We sat in the coach, me in the front seat, riding backward, right across from Annabelle, who was sharing the rear seat with Coop, facing forward. No one else was traveling with us, so we had the roomy coach to ourselves; I'd ridden with as many as a dozen folks jammed into such a space.

Nonetheless, it soon became apparent the coach was too small to contain these three personalities.

"Bert here has aspirations," Annabelle said, eyeing me as the fingers of my left hand skillfully manipulated the deck, "of one day being a card player."

"It's Bret," I said. "And I don't play at it. I work at it."

"A pity," Coop said.

"What is?" I asked.

He snorted. "A fine-looking, strapping young man like yourself, wasting his life away as a tinhorn gambler."

"I'm no tinhorn," I said, fumbled the cards, and had to use two hands to salvage the shuffle, "and I never gamble."

"Bert claims poker isn't gambling," she said with a giddy little laugh.

Coop gave her a warm smile, then looked solemnly, disapprovingly, toward me. "What is it, then, if not gambling?"

"Poker is people," I said.

That was a new one on Annabelle; she took her eyes off her frontier savior and watched me, my one-handed shuffle back in form.

"People?" she asked, her tone trying to sound sarcastic but coming off mostly curious.

I grinned. "It's like my ole pappy used to say. 'If you know poker, you know people. And if you know people, you got the whole dang world lined up in your sights.' "

Coop's expression remained disapproving, but shifted

some into pity. "As *my* late father—a reverend—was wont to say, 'As the twig is bent, so grows the tree.' "

"I'd advise you not to dishonor my ole pappy," I warned him, "else you might *ruffle* me."

He thought about that, but said nothing.

Annabelle put on a wounded-dove expression, even as her eyelids fluttered like hummingbird wings. "I hope you're not *too* disapproving of games of chance, Coop. . . . I've been known, now and then, to indulge in a hand of cards myself."

"I can't rightly say I approve of women gambling," Coop said.

I let out a short laugh. "That's the first thing you've said my pappy would agree with."

Coop gave me a quick glare, then, turning to Annabelle, his expression blossomed back into a smile. "But in my line of work, a man can't be completely ignorant of games of chance."

The Southern belle was interested. "And pray what line of work might that be, sir?"

His response was quiet, dignified, and (of course) modest.

"Lawman," he said.

"*Marshal* Zane Cooper," Annabelle said breathlessly, eyes narrowing as she made the connection. "Why, I believe I've heard of you!"

A shy little smile peeked out from under the handlebar mustache. "That is possible, ma'am."

"I'll just bet you're the best there is," she said, her voice oozing both syrupy Southern charm and awe. Her expression probably was similarly awestruck, but I couldn't see it: I had closed my eyes on this nonsense, to better concentrate on the Maverick shuffle.

"Well, that's not for me to say," Coop replied humbly.

"You know," I said, my eyes still closed, "I just can't quite place your accent, Mrs. Bransford."

"Don't be ridiculous, sir," Coop said, almost gruffly. "It's a Southern accent!"

Keen observations like this separate the lawmen from the boys.

"What I mean is," I said, and opened my eyes to look into the frown that I knew would be pinching her pretty face, "just which part of the South to do you hail from?"

Her smile was as radiant as it was bogus. "Have either of you gentlemen ever been to Mobile?"

"Can't say as I have, ma'am," Coop said.

"Not that I recall," I said.

She nodded. "Well, I hail from Mobile."

"Mo-*bile*?" I said. "I thought you said Mo-*line*."

"That's in Illinois," Coop said to me irritably. "That's hardly the South."

She tilted her head so that I could see her scowl but Coop couldn't.

"Silly me," I said. "You must have meant Mobile, *Alabama*—why, I been there lots of times."

"Small world," Coop offered.

I grinned and shook my head. "Bet we know lots of the same people, Mrs. Bransford. For example, did you ever meet . . . oh. Excuse me—ladies first. *You* start."

Suddenly Annabelle buried her head in Coop's strong shoulder. Her tremulous voice revealed her to be near tears: "I've tried so very hard to forget that terrible place."

He was patting her back and, yes, saying, "There, there, child."

She gazed up at him, and I had to hand it to her: she'd actually worked up some tears, and her cute little chin was all crinkly.

Bravo.

"I . . . I . . . endured such a horrendous personal tragedy in that sinful city. I beg you gentlemen to grant a lady the privilege of *not* discussin' it, further."

"Not a word more shall be spoken," Coop pronounced.

I had dug out a handkerchief and was dabbing my eyes.

Now it was Coop who scowled at me. "A woman's suffering is not a fit source for a man's amusement . . . Bert."

I just scowled right back at him. I had a feeling he would have ordered me to take the next stage out of town if I wasn't already on it.

"Timberr!" came a quavery voice from above, the unmistakable croak of our corpselike driver.

The splash of the ferryboat ramp in the water was followed by the lunge of the coach, rocking on its fore and aft leather-covered coiled-steel springs as the horses trotted forward. The hollow, measured clip-clop of their shod hooves on first the deck, then the ramp, was followed by the splattering of water as the animals took us and the coach that bore us up the riverbank.

Soon the coach was rolling along the valley road, trace chains clanking, our driver cursing and commanding his team, apparently singling out the leader ("Hi, Ollie! Hi!"), doing his best to keep up a constant speed as we wound through majestic stone formations, big wheels pummeling the twin ruts that were the road. In the blue heat-haze of the horizon, miragelike mountains looked on stoically as our coach weaved through the boulder- and cactus-strewn desert desolation.

I played a few rounds of Maverick solitaire on my saddlebag—making five pat poker hands out of a randomly dealt twenty-five cards; unlikely as it sounds, a far easier brand of solitaire to win at than the garden-variety version—and tried not to pay much attention as Annabelle flirted shamelessly with the Great Man of the West.

She had wheedled several tales of selfless valor in pursuit of frontier justice out of the old boy, though truth be told, she didn't have to wheedle very hard.

"*Eight* men?" she gasped. "All of them outlaws? All of them armed to the teeth? And you faced them down alone? I mean, how could anyone . . . even *you* . . ."

"I was the hired representative of law and order in that vicinity." His chin jutted; his lips barely moved when he quietly added: "When a man gives his word to do his job, he does it."

She had her hands clasped together. "But you must have been afraid."

He grinned a little. "Of course I was, Miss Annabelle. Feeling fear doesn't make a man a coward. It's givin' *in* to it that does."

She glanced over at me with hooded eyes and mild contempt. "Mr. *Maverick* doesn't *believe* in bravery."

"Now, Mrs. Bransford," I said affably, "don't misrepresent me. I merely said bravery was overrated. As my ole pappy used to say—"

Coop interrupted. "I just realized something, young man."

"Oh? What's that?"

"You, sir, are everything I detest."

I shrugged. "Then I must be doing something right."

Annabelle, that pillar of ethics, was shaking her head woefully. "Where would the world be if *everyone* were like you?"

"Oh, the world would be just fine. More poker, less violence. Before brother Bart and me went off to war, our pappy said, 'Sons—if either one of you comes back with a medal, I'll kill you both with my bare hands.' Cultivating any other attitude would be disrespectful to my heritage."

Mildly astonished, Annabelle asked, "You were in the war, Mr. Maverick?"

I nodded.

"Blue or gray, sir?" Coop asked.

"We started out gray, wound up galvanized Yankees. Bart and me got captured early on, and had to choose between rottin' in a Yankee prison, or comin' West to help the Union curtail the Indians."

"And after the war?" she asked. She'd started out needling me, but now seemed genuinely interested.

I shuffled the cards, two-handed this time. "Scouted a while, brought in Geronimo once, then changed my mind and helped him get free."

"Why?" she asked, stunned.

I shrugged. "Maybe he belonged free."

She was studying me in a searching kind of way.

Coop was just looking out his window, though there was little to see but the dust fanned up by the running horses.

"I don't believe a word of that," she said.

"Sometimes I have a little trouble believin' it myself," I admitted.

I was asleep.

Dreaming I was riding a bucking bronco, an odd dream for someone who had done so little cowpunching, but in a dream, you don't question. You just ride the bronc.

Then someone was shaking us, not just me, but the horse I was riding, too.

I woke with the taste of dust thick in my mouth, and the pretty but startled-looking face of Annabelle Bransford was close enough for me to worry about what my breath must smell like.

But she wasn't worried. Not about my breath, that is.

"Do you think our driver's found a shortcut?" she asked.

It was a reasonable question, considering that the bucking bronco I'd been riding in my dream seemed to have been inspired by the very out-of-control stagecoach I was seated on.

The stage was damn near flying down the twin-rutted path, rocking crazily on its fore and aft springs, hoofbeats pounding up an all-encompassing dust storm that—along with the lack of any calling out or cursing from our driver above—indicated the team of horses was running as free and wild as an Oregon wind.

Coop had been sleeping, too, and the jarring of the

coach, which the springs could barely soften, as well as Annabelle's shrill questioning, woke him with a start.

Rough, rocky country was streaking by us, barely visible through the dust, but the whine of the wheels in the ruts and their scream against the gray rock closing in on us told the story.

As the coach jolted along, I leaned out one window, and Coop another, on the other side. We had to hang halfway out, but we saw the same thing: our corpselike driver sitting slumped over in his seat. He was nodding at us, but I don't think he was agreeing with anything in particular; in fact, it was pretty obvious he had finally lived up to his appearance.

If "lived" is the word.

I couldn't see if he had hold of the reins or not. I wasn't sure it mattered.

I hauled myself back in.

Coop had done the same. His eyes hard and bright, he said, "I don't think that jasper is sleepin.' "

"Neither do I."

Annabelle was clutching the leather tug strap by the window, but she was bouncing up and down like an out-of-control jack-in-the-box just the same.

Of course, so were Coop and me.

"You climb up there," Coop hollered, "and stop the stage!"

"I don't think I want to do that," I said.

He jerked a thumb toward the window, and his expression was grave. "The back wheel on my side is comin' loose! If it falls off, we're all of us deader than Lincoln. Understand?"

I nodded, or maybe it was just the jostling of the runaway stage.

"Now I'll climb out and secure that wheel," Coop said, "and you go up and take the reins of this buggy. Don't think about it, boy, just *do* it!"

"Why don't *you* do it," I said, "and I'll secure the wheel."

"No," Coop said sternly, as the coach bounced all of us like balls, "you do it!"

I was clutching the tug strap by the window for dear life, when Annabelle slapped my hand as if I were a naughty child.

"*You* do it!" she said, eyes flaring. "You're the younger man!"

In this instance, Coop didn't seem slighted by the remark in the least.

And that was when I did a damn fool thing.

I opened the door.

Clouds of alkali dust rose like smoke from a blazing fire, and I kept my feet precariously balanced on the hanging-steel step plate, but I was not trying to get in or out of the coach, but up and over it. Coughing, squinting, as the dust swirled around me, I groped, my fingers seeking purchase on the steel railing above.

Then I had hold!

I gripped it and stepped off the steel-plate step and pulled myself up. I had a good strong hold, and if I could just blink the dust out of my eyes and get my damn bearings—

Whump!

We must've hit a hell of a rut, sailing through this rough terrain, because that good strong hold gave way, and I was sliding back down over the ribbed, paneled surface of the coach, my hands finally catching the lip of the window sill. My feet scraped the hard-dirt floor of the roadbed, throwing more dust, before I swung my legs up and under the coach and caught the wooden undercarriage.

If I couldn't go up, maybe I could go *under*.

Catching a breath that was partly air, mostly dirt, I let go of the sill and my legs supported me while I slipped under the curved body of the coach and rode its framework even as it pitched and rocked along the rutted road, the pounding horses' hooves churning up miniature dust devils.

Somehow I maneuvered under the coach, along the skeletal wooden structure that supported the axles, and worked my way to the rear, where I scaled the leather webbing of the back luggage carrier like an awkward spider, and got first one hand on that roof's steel railing, and then the other hand—

Whump!

Another rut, but this one helped! It flipped me up onto the roof, and I landed hard, on my back, all the wind *whoosh*ing out, but I didn't let loose, I still had that damn railing.

Whump!

As the coach lurched and jolted, I climbed across the roof, over luggage strapped there, pausing to look on Coop's side of the vehicle—*where was he?* I prayed the old bastard hadn't fallen to his death, trying to repair that wheel. Maybe he'd done it already, and had climbed back in. . . .

Or maybe there wasn't anything wrong with that wheel,

and it had been just a con to send me out here on this scenic tour.

But there was no time to ponder that. Instead, I crawled up over the luggage compartment, to the driver's seat—only it wasn't that easy. The buckboard seat was several feet below, and getting down there had to be timed just right, otherwise if we hit a rut while I was trying, I could end up going ass-over-tea-kettle into that team of sweating, muscle-bunching horses.

And then down under the steel-rimmed wheels.

The driver couldn't help me. He was a full-fledged corpse now, all right, sprawled in his seat, his only motion that of the bouncing coach. At least the reins were still looped through his slack hands.

The air up here wasn't as dusty. That was good. I grabbed some, and lowered myself, and *whump!*, another deep rut sent me careening through space, and I clutched at the air, clutched at anything, anything at all, praying for a hold . . .

My fingers touched cloth, gripped it, clutched some more, and then I had hold of something, had hold of *him*, the dead driver, and somehow I wrapped my arms around him, hugging him, but he was no damn help at all, being dead and all, and he even had the lack of courtesy to start falling off the coach himself, sliding on the smooth wooden seat under the pressure of my grip.

Hoofbeats thundering in my ears, I was hanging off the coach now, holding on to only a corpse who was about to fall off himself; so the hell with him! I lunged for the railing that circled his seat, caught it, and, as the rampaging coach suddenly tilted the other way, the driver, reins still loosely looped around his hands, started sliding the other way, off the seat.

Then I was on the wooden bench of it, riding shotgun-less shotgun on a stagecoach whose dead driver was about to fall off.

"You're not going anywhere!" I screamed, not with those reins in his limp paws he wasn't, and he didn't say a word when I grabbed him and reeled him back in, sitting him beside me in his rightful position.

"Behave!" I yelled at him, as I fumbled with his slack fingers, prying loose the reins. The stage hit another rut, just deep enough to jar the corpse closer to me, and suddenly his arms were around my neck, affectionately.

I didn't pay any attention—I had to get those damn reins in my hands, and then I had them, I *had* them.

I shouldered the driver to one side, screaming, "Sit there and shut up!" and, a leather ribbon in either hand, held good and tight, I hollered, "Whoa!"

They responded to my command.

But not exactly as I'd hoped.

The cantankerous equine bastards, whipped up in a foaming frenzy as they were, picked up speed, hooves pounding furiously.

"Just *whoa*, goddamnit!"

Their next burst of speed damn near pulled me off the seat and onto their backs.

I scrambled back into position, my butt bouncing on the buckboard, clutched those reins as tight as I could, and yanked back on them, calling upon every muscle and sinew I had developed in a life devoted assiduously to avoiding hard work.

And I knew enough not to holler "Whoa!" again.

What else had my late compadre here used to get their attention? I thought back to the ferryboat. Maybe it was worth a try.

"Tim-berrrrr!" I yelled, as I pulled back on the reins.

And I'll be damned.

It was working. The beasts were slowing and, once their pace had ebbed, they gave in to their exhaustion, clopping to a leisurely halt.

For a few moments I just sat there, reins slack in my hands, exhausted and yet exhilarated. My heart was pounding; my breath heaving. The driver, slumped next to me, was having a quiet moment, too.

Below, at my left, Coop stepped down out of the coach and, in most gentlemanly manner, helped Annabelle down.

That old buzzard, I thought and, with no more heed than that, hopped down off the stage.

I guess I should've been paying attention.

In the swirling dust, in all the commotion, I hadn't noticed, I hadn't realized, that we'd come to a stop along the edge of a drop-off.

A sheer drop-off, at that, down the rocky face of a canyon. Oh, it wasn't as deep as the Grand Canyon. In fact, not near that deep. Just deep enough to crush every bone in a man's body, should he decide to fall off the edge.

Which was a decision I was trying to make, standing on the rimrock edge with my back to it, a howling wind blowing up the canyon behind me, beckoning me, as my arms frantically flailed. I dared not look behind me at the long fall that awaited as I windmilled, my vision filled with the sight of Coop watching safely, several yards away, a reassuring arm around Annabelle's waist.

Her expression was distraught; she had her face covered with a gloved hand, peeking through her fingers at my teetering predicament.

"Aren't you going to help him?" she asked Coop.

"After all the lad has worked so hard to accomplish," Coop said grandly, "he would only resent it. In the long run, he'll live to thank me."

Then I had my balance, and stumbled forward onto solid ground, pitching forward, landing on my face, raising one last dust cloud.

A powerful hand reached into my view

"Allow me to lend a helpin' hand," Coop said.

I glared up at him. "You've done way too much already." Then I got to my feet, dusting myself off, saying, "I mean, fixing the wheel and all. Otherwise we'd have been killed."

"Seems I was wrong," Coop said. "Wheel was fine all along."

He leaned in and whispered in my ear. "Somebody had to stay behind and protect the little lady, son."

Flush with indignation, Annabelle raised her chin, her fists on either side of her narrow waist. "Marshal Cooper was doing you a *favor*."

My eyes popped. "A favor?"

She nodded, once. "He was helping you feel better about yourself. And don't you feel better, now that you've done something brave?"

I stood frozen for a moment. Then I wiped the mask of alkali off my face with my hands and went over to Coop, and gave him the sunny smile.

"I understand now," I said. "This was for my benefit. Building up my character."

"Exactly." Coop looked skyward, smiled nostalgically. "How well I remember my first runaway stage . . . there's a knack to it, you know."

"Oh, I'm learning. Funny." I shook my head. "You'd think I'd be mad."

Annabelle had gotten my gun belt from the stagecoach. "Here, Bret."

Not "Bert," for a change; she seemed so very proud of me.

"But I'm not. Not mad in the least." I strapped the holstered .44 on, tied it down on my leg. "One little thing, though."

Coop beamed at his pupil. "Yes, lad?"

I drew the gun—bushed as I was, my lightning draw was just fine—and thumbed back the hammer with a nasty *click,* and he looked down the barrel, with those beady eyes damn near crossed.

"Try not to help me again," I said.

7

Dangers, Toils, and Snares

By the time the shovel patted the last of the dirt down, the sun was low in a sky streaked with purple and orange, and our shadows fell long over the grave of our nameless driver. I put the shovel, which Coop and I had traded off using, back in the tool chest in the stagecoach boot, while Coop pressed stones in the face of the grave, making a cross.

Both of us were a mite dirty and sweat-soaked, but should a similar fate befall one of us, I'm sure we both hoped the next wayfarer would do us the same kindness.

We stood at the grave, hats in hand, with Annabelle between us.

"Your pa was a reverend, you said," I reminded him. "You say the words."

Coop nodded and recited the Lord's prayer. I joined in. Annabelle, about a third of the way through, did, too.

"I suppose," Coop said, awkwardly, "somebody ought to say something nice about the deceased."

"How do we know *he* was nice?" Annabelle grumbled, mislaying her Southern accent for a moment. Her face was harsh with irritation. "We don't know a damn thing about the old codger, 'cept he up and died on us and come close to getting us killed."

Coop cast a disappointed look in her direction.

"Well, we don't!" she said, with a defensive wag of her head and a toss of her curls. "He didn't even have a name in his wallet . . . just that list of bordellos."

"The flesh is weak," Coop said.

"It's weak, and I'm hungry," she said. "And you said we should try to make that way station before dark."

I was hungry too, and, like Annabelle, I'm not much for standing on ceremony, or for taking life too seriously. But death? That was something else again.

I began to sing. "Amazing Grace, how sweet the sound . . ."

My voice echoed across the barren landscape; didn't sound half bad. All of a sudden Coop joined in.

". . . that saved a wretch like me," we sang.

In harmony yet. The old boy didn't have a bad voice, either.

The harshness left Annabelle's face, putting the

prettiness back, and I could tell she was sorry about what she'd said. And, that our harmony moved her.

". . . I once was lost," we all three sang, "but now am found . . ."

She had a lovely voice, high and clear and flowing, like a mountain stream, though she was a mite shaky on the words. She dropped out during the part that went: ". . . was bound, but now I'm free."

But when we came up on the next verse, she was right with us, and we sang like we'd been singing together for years; there wasn't a country church in the land that wouldn't have claimed us.

"Through many dangers, toils, and snares," we harmonized, voices ringing out over the countryside, "I have already come. But Grace has led me safe thus far. And Grace will lead me home . . ."

As the echo of our sweet song died out, we said a silent prayer, each in our own way, muttered an "Amen" or two, and left our fellow traveler behind in his new earthen home.

Then we headed for Gap Station to get some grub and bed down for the night.

The next morning, when we left the way station well-fed and equally well-rested, the three of us decided to ride up top, together. Annabelle liked the idea of the air and the scenery, and also didn't cotton to riding alone in the coach. Coop and I switched off on the driving, and both of us got the hang of it pretty quick; the horses were behaving themselves, and the rutted road held no surprises.

Not until we rounded a bend and saw the little wagon train.

The sound of sobbing made a lonely plaintive song accompanying the pathetic sight of four Conestoga wagons, their canvas coverings burned away, their boatlike wooden frames scorched and still smoldering. Women and children were huddling around their fallen menfolk, weeping and wailing; the men appeared to be wounded, not killed, which was some solace. Several saddle horses and oxen lay dead in the sun, entertaining the flies.

Life on the frontier was frequently hard for settlers like these. People drowned at river crossings. A boil on a child's neck led to a fevered death. Cholera, dysentery. Wagons breaking down. Animals dead of snakebite. But none of nature's travails could top the sort of tragedy man could deliver upon man.

It looked like an Indian raid. Years ago, in my scouting days, I'd seen similar sad scenes. The only thing that compared in heartbreak was what the bluecoats did, from time to time, to a helpless Indian village.

But those days were long over. Fewer and fewer prairie schooners were making their lumbering way across this hard country, and there were no hostile Indians left at all—thanks to people like me.

I pulled back on the reins, bringing the stagecoach to a stop, and Coop vaulted to the ground like a man half his age, practically sprinting over to the ruined wagons.

Momentarily free from Coop's supervision, Annabelle got a flask out from somewhere and took a long pull; the smell of whiskey was unmistakable. Wiping her mouth with the back of a delicate hand, she passed the flask my way, but I shook my head no.

"Sorry," she said. "Slipped my mind, your avoidance of hard liquor and hard work."

Coop was patiently talking to two women whose tattered calico dresses and white bonnets blew in the dry breeze. Even at this distance, you could see the two were mother and daughter. Coop gestured toward us, and began walking the two settler women our way.

I helped Annabelle down and we met them at the roadside.

Coop gave a gentlemanly introductory sweep of an arm. "This is Mrs. Colbert and her daughter, Millicent."

"Condolences on your misfortune, ma'am," I said, taking my hat off.

"Indian attack, they say," Coop said.

The mother, a raw-boned woman in her fifties, her sky-blue eyes a beautiful misnomer in her prematurely time-ravaged face, was just this side of hysterical.

"It was horrible, so horrible," she said. "Those savages snuck up on us and . . . and . . ."

She couldn't find the words, but her eyes filled it in.

But I said, "All due respect, ma'am—it wasn't Indians."

Her frown was fierce. "Well, they were all gussied up in war paint, a' screamin' and whoopin' and hollerin'."

"There are no hostiles in these parts, ma'am . . ."

She didn't want to hear it; she shivered and held to her bosom her sniffling daughter—a comely girl in her early twenties—as if the child were a child. Annabelle began to question them, gently, about the raid, and Coop took me aside.

"I told 'em we'd take 'em back to Crystal River," he said. "I believe we can squeeze the whole passel of 'em inside, and on top of, the coach."

"That's backtrackin' a little, ain't it?"

"Just a day."

"I got a poker game to get to . . ."

The mother had started to cry. Coop was looking at her, cow-eyed, and I knew I'd lost.

"They shot our menfolk," she was wailing, "and they set torches to our wagons, and slaughtered our horses and oxen—"

"I'll just take one horse," I whispered to Coop. "They can spare a saddle off one of those dead animals, and you can—"

But the woman's voice was climbing in volume, as her description of the atrocities continued: "—and stole the wagon with all of our money—"

"Money?" I said.

I went to the poor woman.

She was sobbing again. "My baby's music box, it's gone . . . gone forever . . ."

Finally the daughter spoke: "And they even took my weddin' dress! What could they want my weddin' dress for, Mama?"

"Excuse me," I said. "What was that part about money, again?"

"Maverick," Coop said, his voice low and resonant and preacherly. "Have you no decency, sir?"

I took the woman's hand, and patted it. "I know this

is a difficult time," I said, quietly understanding. "How *much* money, exactly?"

Even Annabelle seemed disgusted with me.

"You're a beast!" she said. Then she stepped between me and the womem, mocking me, her voice seeping with spurious sympathy: "How *much* money, exactly?"

And mother and daughter, clutching each other in sorrow, sniffling, choking back sobs, answered us in unison, "Thirty thousand dollars."

Annabelle looked at me, stunned; somebody might have cold-cocked her. I probably wore the same expression.

We pressed in on the two women, both of us asking them questions so fast and so intensely that it knocked the sorrow right out of them, replacing it with fear.

"Stop!" I yelled, and Annabelle shut up.

The two women were huddled together, trembling with fright.

"Ma'am," I said calmly, doing my best to settle them (and myself, and Annabelle) down, "if I can get your thirty thousand dollars back, is it worth ten percent to you?"

Quick as a jackrabbit, the mother said, "Five."

"Mother," sniffled the girl who'd lost her music box and wedding gown, "give them anything they want!"

Coop, standing to one side, arms folded, was shaking his head in solemn disapproval.

"Vultures," he said, by way of editorial comment.

The raw-boned old gal was neither grieving nor frightened, now; merely shrewd. "You really think you could get our money back? It's everything we have . . . everything we *had* . . ."

I gave her a confident version of the sunny smile, and started to reply, but Annabelle butted in, first.

"You *bet* we could!" she said.

I frowned at her. "What's this 'we' business? I don't remember taking on a partner—"

"For ten percent," the rawboned gal said, her arms folded like an Indian chief's. "I want you to make those savages *pay* for what they done!"

I was glad to hear the ten percent figure, but I had to tell her the truth.

"Ma'am, believe me. I was an Indian scout when I was little more than your daughter's age. And there are no—repeat, *no*—hostiles in this part of the country."

A *boom* seemed to put a period at the end of my sentence, but that *boom* was followed by another, and another, until my sentence was turned into a question by a tempo-building cadence, echoing down from the hills.

Indian war drums.

8

Prairie Flower

The tracks were fresh. There were no signs of rain, meaning anything but the most recent horse or cattle tracks would either be obliterated or cracked with age. These tracks were only hours old.

"They're on shod ponies," I said, moving through the brush on foot, Annabelle just behind me. A few steps to the rear, also on foot, Coop led the three stagecoach horses we'd saddled up. Since my eyes were cast downward, Coop was keeping a constant, moving lookout. At the moment, I didn't mind having him along at all.

And he had no critical comments on my tracking

skills. The old boy could recognize a man who could follow a woodtick over a solid rock.

On the other hand, there was the third member of our little tracking party.

"What do you mean, they shot their ponies?" she asked incredulously.

"They didn't *shoot* their ponies," I said. "Their ponies are shod."

"Oh. Shod!"

We kept moving, brittle brush crunching under our feet.

"So they've been shod," Annabelle said. "So what?"

"So, Indians don't shod their horses."

"Maybe these Indians stole some 'shod' horses."

"It's *not* Indians."

She wrinkled her pretty face. "What is it with you and Indians, anyway? They're just filthy savages."

I stopped and smiled pleasantly. "You know, Annabelle, come to think of it, you're right. They're just a pack of thieves and savages, and ungrateful ones, at that."

"Ungrateful?"

I moved on, eyes down, my eyes tracing the impressions in the brush. The earth seemed less arid here; for miles, we'd seen only greasewood, dried grass, flaming ocotillo, and various cacti, the sort of stubborn-cuss flora that could take hold even in desert sand. But the world was greening up some.

"Ungrateful," I said. "After all, didn't we give 'em smallpox?"

"Very funny," she said.

"But then, I figure they deserved it for being on our

land when we got here. Speaking of people bein' where they don't belong, what exactly are you doing here?"

"We're partners. Fifty-fifty."

"Suppose we take that giant leap," I said, stopping for a moment. "Suppose we say we *are* partners. Who determined the split? Your tracking abilities leave somethin' to be desired."

From behind us, Coop put in his two cents: "Fifty-fifty sounds fair to me."

I glowered back at him. "And just how do you see *your* part in this? Three partners don't add up to fifty-fifty."

He gave me a narrow-eyed, suspicious look. "Someone has to keep you children honest. If you should prove successful, someone has to see to it those fine brave ladies get their money back."

One of the horses he was leading whinnied. I believe he was expressing my opinion.

I pressed on. The brush was turning into a thicket. If these "Indians" thought they could lose us in here, they really were dumb savages.

Annabelle scurried up to my side.

"No fifty-fifty split," I said.

"Then we'll make it sixty-forty, if you're going to be bellicose about it."

I just looked at her. "Belli . . . what?"

"Bellicose. Or perhaps that's too harsh—possibly 'recalcitrant' says it better."

I looked back at Coop, who didn't know what the hell she was talking about, either.

She touched her bosom. "Education, gentlemen. It's something civilized people partake of."

"Fancy words, Annabelle," I said, "but they ain't worth sixty-forty. What did you plan to do for your share, besides recite the dictionary?"

The thicket floor was a tangle, and she was holding on to my arm; I guess I didn't mind.

"I'm going to help," she said.

"You're going to help?"

"Yes. For a one thing, you're not all alone out here. You have someone to bounce ideas off—"

She chose this moment to hook the toe of one but-toned-up shoe under a dead branch, losing her balance, and lurching forward, into me, grabbing at me. Struggling to regain her footing, she clutched my gunbelt, and one of her hands sought support on the .44 itself.

The sixgun fired once, shaking the thicket and star-tling the horses, not to mention me. While Coop settled the shying horses, I just stood there staring at the woman, gunsmoke drifting up to tickle my nostrils.

I supposed if she'd shot my toe off or anything, I'd have noticed. Glancing down, I saw the small black hole bored into the earth.

"Bouncing what off?" I asked.

Her expression was the offspring of a smile and a grimace. "Make it seventy-thirty, then," she asked timidly.

We pressed on. The thicket was getting denser, bushes joined by trees, but just beyond, things got desolate again. I ducked under a branch.

"Big tracker," she muttered, as she ducked. "Follow a couple of horse tracks—anybody could do that."

I stopped, turned to her, and pointed to the sky,

where a hawk was gliding effortlessly over the landscape.

"See that?"

"Well, of course."

"But do you know what it *means*? In this situation? What it tells us about the men we're tracking?"

She frowned in thought, and her mouth puckered, as if she were trying to think of something intelligent to say, or maybe wanted a kiss. Finally, she shrugged, and said, "No. What does it mean?"

"Nothing."

A disgusted sigh seeped through her teeth like escaping steam.

"But you didn't know that," I pointed out.

"Of course I did! I knew it didn't mean anything; you're the one that implied it had significance—"

"Oh! More educated words to justify my givin' you ten percent."

"Ten percent! You cheap bas—"

"Children!" It was Coop's voice, and it was scolding. The horses he was leading nodded in agreement; they thought we were idiots, too.

Pausing there for a moment, returning Annabelle's glare, I heard something. Something very faint. Something only the ears of somebody who'd spent months, even years of his life out in barren lands like these could discern.

I could smell it, too.

And it wasn't Annabelle's lilac water.

It was just plain water. And it was where the "savages" we were tracking would wind up for the day. The sun was lowering in the sky, and they'd put plenty of miles between themselves and their victims—who were no threat to come after them, anyway.

No. They would bed down by the water.

I moved to the edge of the thicket, knelt at the ground, put my ear to the sandy earth. The faint music of flowing water called to me.

Annabelle, thinking I was still pulling her leg (not an unpleasant notion, actually), leaned over and smiled with sweet sarcasm. "Let me guess. The Indians in Montana are having a powwow."

"Shhh!" I was trying to listen. Then I whispered, "It's not Indians."

I smoothed a place in the sand and stretched out on my back; it was a nice shady spot, here at the edge of the thicket. Rocks and trees; good shelter—good cover. I could still hear the music. I closed my eyes.

"What are you doing?" Her voice was hushed. Her sarcasm had been replaced with curiosity about my tracking techniques.

Coop knew. He was already tying the horses to a tree.

"Takin' a nap," I said. "When the sun starts goin' down, I'll sneak up on them. And it's *not* Indians."

Coop agreed that he should stay behind with Annabelle, and I agreed to come back for them before I did anything rash. Whether they cared about me, or the settler women's money, I'll leave for you to determine.

On horseback, I followed the edge of the thicket, pausing at times to climb down and put my ear to the earth. Gradually, the terrain got both greener and rockier, and the music got louder until it was unmistakably a waterfall.

Then the gentle breeze brought me a present: the faint, acrid aroma of smoke, teasing my nostrils. I dismounted, leading the horse—Ollie, the stagecoach lead, with whom I was already forging a bond (I whistled, he came)—over rocky terrain as the rush of the waterfall continued to draw me nearer.

Then there was more music, but not the flowing of water. It was the tinkling, carefree, and yet somehow melancholy sound of a music box playing, "Oh, Dem Golden Slippers." Always a big Indian favorite. . . .

I tied Ollie to a small tree, then whispered to him: "Quiet . . . and stay that way."

Ollie nodded.

I patted his head. "If you're smarter than me, just keep it to yourself."

And he nodded again.

They were camped by the side of the stream, and had a fire going. The rush of the waterfall over the nearby rocks made their laughter and raucous glee echo. There were six of them, passing whiskey bottles around, some still wearing war paint, others washing the stuff off in the stream. All of them laughing. Some of the "injuns" danced ungainly jigs around the open-lidded wooden box within which a metal disc revolved and played its plink-plunkey tune. Some of them sang.

All of them were white.

When I got back to camp, Annabelle was sort of snuggling against fatherly Coop by a big rock, his arm around her as he rested and she snoozed. Ollie's approaching hoofbeats stirred them both, and they were soon on their feet.

I dismounted and told them what I'd found.

"Come with me," I said to Coop. "It's not much of a ride, and I need a witness."

"A witness?" Annabelle said.

"I need somebody to vouch for me," I said. "To back me up in sayin' these six dwarfs are snow-white."

"You wouldn't want the poor innocent Indians blamed," Annabelle said, mockingly.

"Well, we could pass the blame on to them. I mean, we've spoiled them like damn kids from the beginning. Oh, sure, it's true we poisoned 'em, infected 'em, killed 'em off like we did their buffalo . . . but I say it's their fault for bein' on our land."

I think Annabelle finally got the point. I know Coop did.

"Let's make tracks!" I said. "The way they're whoopin' it up, should be easy pickins. As my ole pappy used to say, 'You don't have to be a prizefighter to lick a liquored man.'"

That perked Annabelle up. "This could be exciting!"

"Now, wait," I said. "I didn't mean—"

She got fluttery again, though by now even Coop must have seen through it. "You wouldn't leave a delicate prairie flower like myself out here in the wasteland alone, would you?"

Coop was at her side, hat in hand. "Comin' along could be a mite dangerous, too, ma'am."

I was mounting my horse.

Her lilting voice intoned a familiar refrain. "Couldn't be as dangerous as bein' a married woman in the presence of the most overwhelmin'ly attractive man on the face of this earth."

Did she really think I was going to fall for that line of bull again. Flattering—and accurate—as it might be?

I turned to comment, but then I realized she wasn't speaking to me.

She was gazing into the eyes of Marshal Zane Cooper, and he was gazing right back.

And the only smile "on the face of this earth" sillier than hers, was his.

9

Faint Hearts and Flushes

We tied our horses up at the same tree I'd used before. Twilight had laid its gentle, cooling, blue-tinged hand on the rocky hillside. The sound of nearby rushing water mingled with the tinkle-tink of the music box. "Silver Threads Among the Gold" was playing now; these "savages" apparently knowing instinctively how to change the steel disc on the newfangled contraption.

I was leading Coop and Annabelle down the rocky slope toward the brush edging the stream, when the refined Mrs. Bransford whispered her dumbest question yet: "Could you teach me how to be a great poker player?"

"You mean, *now*?"

Her eyes were as wide and naive as a child's. "Well . . . suppose you're dead tomorrow, and aren't there to answer my questions."

"Yeah—*then* how would I feel?"

"Can you?"

"Make you a great poker player? Not if I lived to be Coop's ripe old age."

Coop's glare meant to be withering, but I basked in it.

"But working on your 'tells' would make you *better*," I whispered. We were still moving forward, accompanied by the metallic plinkety-plankety of the music box. "Poker's about when, and *how*, to bluff. But you got two dead giveaways. First, you touch your thumbnail to the nail of your little finger. Second—"

"Shut up," Coop said, his voice flat as a mesa.

He had a point.

We stayed quiet after that—except for when Annabelle's shoe brushed a stone and sent it skittering; we froze, but nothing happened, nobody came looking. Annabelle mouthed a silent "sorry," and we crept on.

Soon we were huddled in the bushes, drawing them back just enough to see the campsite, which was up and away from the stream bank on flat, dusty ground. Dusk had darkened to night now, but the flow of the campfire (and a generous hunk of moon) showed us everything we needed to see. Six ornery-looking characters, some still smeared with war paint, were snuggled 'neath the blankets of their rolled-out bedrolls. Scattered here and there were the whiskey bottles, the emptying of which had set these raiders to snoring.

Their six horses were tied to trees nearby, while by the dwindling fire, the spring-driven music box was slowly winding down, making its sad song sadder and sadder.

"See the paint on their faces?" I whispered to Coop.

"Two of 'em," he allowed.

"You'll vouch for that?"

He nodded.

"That's all the proof we'll need," I said.

"Could just be some drunken cowpokes havin' a frolic," Coop pointed out.

"No," I said impatiently, "they're the raiders. You hear that damn music box, don't you? Remember what that old gal said about them taking her daughter's music box, don't you?"

"Circumstantial evidence," he said, just like a lawman. "Proof is identification. Right now, you got so much air . . . Hot air, at that."

Once again, he had a point.

I looked out at the six slumbering men. Then I looked at Coop. "We can bring 'em in easy. We got surprise on our side."

" 'We'? That's a new concept for you, isn't it, son? Seems to me, this is *your* show."

"You'd let me face down six men? By myself?"

"I'm convinced deep inside your buffoonish facade, there's a real man struggling to get out."

Annabelle leaned in to the conversation. "Don't worry . . . they're asleep, and obviously drunk. Why, Coop here brought in eight outlaws dead sober."

"He's always sober," I said.

"She didn't mean that way," Coop said, as Annabelle said, "I meant the *outlaws* were dead sober."

And our conversation had turned just a mite loud for sneaking up on an enemy camp, particularly Annabelle's contribution, which is why both Coop and I clamped our hands over her sweet mouth.

Even as we did this, one of those six owlhoots, a skinny, war-painted one, was rousing; he'd heard something in the bushes, it seemed. How could that have happened? He leaned on an elbow and looked right toward where we hoped the bushes were shielding us from sight.

He reached under his blanket, and came back with a sixgun.

Then he flipped his blanket back and stood, looking around ominously, war-paint–smudged face hovering over his red long johns. He looked so ridiculous I might have laughed, if it weren't for the .45 Remington in his hand.

Then something else caught his attention: a whiskey bottle he damn near tripped over. He bent down, shook it some, and grinned, hearing the slosh of a generous remainder of tarantula juice. He raised the bottle to his lips, threw a big swig down his gullet, then returned to his beddings, where he sat finishing it off before crawling back under his blankets.

After a while, I whispered to Coop, "You'll back me up, if there's trouble?"

"Count on it," he said. Dead serious.

"I'll whistle, then you come runnin'. Okay?"

"Your lips'll still be puckered and that'll be me at your side."

"None of this 'wheel comin' off' bunkum?"

He seemed offended. "That was about broken bones. This is about dyin'."

Was that supposed to reassure me?

I turned to Annabelle; she looked mighty lovely in the moonlight, but I didn't give a damn about the moonlight.

"Gimme your gun," I said.

She feigned surprise. "How do you even know I have a gun?"

"You're a woman livin' in a world of men. You've got a derringer or somethin' tucked away somewhere."

"What does the fastest draw anybody's ever seen need with a little itsy bitsy ladies' pistol?"

"I need all the bullets I can get. Did you ever consider, maybe I show off that fast draw 'cause in a real fight, when it's *people* I'm aiming at, I . . . just give me your damn gun!"

She withdrew a small pistol from a pocket. It was tiny, but not a derringer: a genuine revolver, giving me five bullets to play with. That was good.

Coop placed a hand on my shoulder and squeezed; his look was one of steely-eyed encouragement. Annabelle squeezed my arm and gazed at me with genuine concern.

"Well," I said. "As my old pappy says, 'Faint heart never filled a flush'."

And I stood up, walked out of the bushes, and into the outlaws' camp.

A couple of them heard me immediately, and the rest of them at least stirred. I had my .44 holstered and my hands held up, waist-high.

"Evenin', gents."

Half a dozen scruffy-looking, long john–wearing cow-pokes, two with smeary war-painted faces, sat up in their bedding and blinked at me like I was something they were dreaming, or maybe a delusion the whiskey conjured.

"Name's Burt"—I *was* nervous—"*Bret* Maverick."

And I gave them the sunny smile.

The six confused faces played a round robin of confusion, looking each to the other.

I moved near the flickering campfire. "Sorry to barge in on you like this, middle of the night. I'm just here to give you one little piece of information . . ."

Confusion was dissolving into suspicion and irritation; could rage be far behind?

". . . right now," I said sunnily, "right at this moment, guns are trained on each and every one of you."

That woke 'em up in a hurry.

But nobody sprang to his feet. They believed what this insane intruder, his voice indicating not a care in the world, had just shared with them; their eyes were furiously searching the bushes and the darkness. They weren't showing their guns, but like the skinny, war-painted jasper who'd almost come looking for us in the bushes, they undoubtedly each had a sixgun or two hidden under their blankets.

"Now, you have a perfect right to know who's out there, and why," I assured them. I pointed to the man nearest me; he had a long white scar on one unshaven cheek and his eyes were dark and burning.

"The man who'll blow your brains out is Marshal

Zane Cooper," I said amiably. "A true legend of the West. I'm sure you've heard of him. As for you . . ."

And I pointed to the next man, a chunky blond who was afraid even before I told him who was poised to kill him.

". . . John Wesley Hardin's got you singled out. He's used to closer-up work, and thought you'd make a good target for distance shootin'. And you . . ."

This was the skinny war-painted owlhoot.

". . . *you* face the ignoble and short-rangin' future of bein' shot by a woman. Of course, not just any woman: Ugly Annie Bransford, chased at an early age out of Mobile, Alabama, they say, for her face stoppin' too many clocks. Twice as repulsive as Calamity Jane, and killed four times as many men."

I made sure I'd spoken loudly and distinctively enough for my audience in the bushes to hear.

"And as for you . . ." I was pointing at the next man, a hatchet-faced character with an eye tic, but then stopped, and just threw up my hands. "You get my meaning. Why this fuss? Seems some Indians attacked some white settlers over near Gap Station. Now *you* know it was Indians, and *I* know it was Indians, but some of these women survivors, they got a mite hysterical and raised the notion it was white men masqueradin' as redskins. Silliest thing I ever heard tell of."

They were looking one to another again; they had skipped rage and gone straight to fear.

I thought I'd best settle them down. "Now, this posse I'm with, we know we're on a fool's mission. Ain't no fool woman who could make positive identification of a man in war paint, on horseback, nohow. So you need to decide . . . do you want to make a ruckus right now, with them that's got you in their gun sights? Or just come peaceable, when all it's gonna cost you is a few hours' beauty sleep."

I was getting to them. But that one with the scar and the hard eyes, he might be a problem.

"Now the reason I'm out here," I said, "is, well, some folks think I can talk pretty good. Not that I don't know my way around a sixgun."

Faint heart never filled a flush.

I demonstrated my lightning draw—and in the flicker of fire- and moonlight, it did look like lightning.

The six men, in their blankets, were gathered around me with the fearful expressions of campers whose leader just scared the tar out of them with one hell of a ghost story.

I spun the .44 back into its holster. Greased lightning, this time.

Folding my arms, casual, taking as unthreatening a posture as a man could assume, I said, "So, fellers—all you got to do is stand up and put your hands on your head. And don't worry—Ugly Annie's seen men in their long johns, before."

They were back to confusion, though the fear wasn't gone, and then the hatchet-faced guy was on his feet, his eye tic twitching up a storm, as he put his hands on top of his head.

Then the chunky blond jasper did the same, locking his fingers on top of his head, and the scar-faced, burning-eyed character sprang to his feet as well.

Only he had a gun in his hand.

And a redheaded varmint was tossing blankets aside to reveal another gun at the ready too.

So I stuck two fingers in my mouth and whistled for Coop to play cavalry. Whistled loud and clear.

But the only thing that happened was the bad guys' half-dozen horses, tied to their trees, lurched forward.

If Coop wasn't coming to the rescue, at least the moment of whinnying from the horses provided just enough distraction for me to dive to safety a fraction of an instant before bullets pounded the ground where I'd been.

I rolled and came up firing, twice, and the redheaded varmint on his knees never made it to his feet, one of my bullets carving my displeasure into his forearm, eliciting a scream and sending his gun flying. He was scrambling after it, but I was scrambling, too, while squeezing one off to reprimand the scar-faced owlhoot who'd started it, my .44 slug crushing his shoulder and sending his gun who-knows-where and him howling to the ground.

Bullets were *whing*ing around me, so I rolled sideways as two more of the raiders—just blurred red shapes in long underwear, one in war paint, blasting away at me—demanded my attention. And I gave it, two shots worth, one each: the hand of one, the knee of the other, eliminating the second, who was crying like a baby from the shattering pain, while the other guy, the war-painted one, had his hand nicked, sending his gun somewhere in the night. He went scurrying after it.

I couldn't help. I was busy, 'cause that pudgy jasper and the hatchet-faced guy, who'd been so cooperative before, had taken their hands off their heads and dropped to the ground to find their weapons.

So I dove again and rolled up on my feet, but the bullets were whining and kicking up dust, and I dove again, making an even harder target of myself. Then I got to one knee and scolded the pudgy boy by putting a bullet in his right thigh, folding him up like a squeeze box, only when I wheeled to let the hatched-faced guy have his, somebody beat me to him.

Two sharp shots, from the bushes, taught him a nasty lesson—the first by cutting a red crease in the guy's gunhand, making him toss the firearm in the air like it was hot, and the second by crunching into his shoulder with a blow that sent him crying out as he dropped to the ground with a dust-raising *thud*.

Maybe the cavalry had come, after all.

No depending on it, though: the redheaded varmint with the bleeding forearm was back for more, holding his sixgun in his left hand, trying his best to aim.

It was almost too easy a shot for me, or at least it seemed that way till I heard the *click* of the hammer falling on an empty chamber.

Out of bullets. *Maverick,* I thought, *you can keep track of 52 cards without trying, but six little bullets elude you. . . .*

I let the sixgun drop and reached around for Annabelle's dainty revolver.

It felt like a toy in my hand, though I didn't have much time to think about that, as the redhead had fired off a round, not very steadily, but a bullet's a bullet. With the redhead's wild gunfire all around me, I jumped back, did a quick somersault, and came up with the tiny gun almost invisible in my hand, firing off one quick dead-solid-perfect shot.

The bullet nailed the redhead in the left shoulder and he cried out in pain and surprise, mostly pain, and dropped his gun.

I looked at the little gun with mild surprise; damn thing actually worked.

But it wasn't over.

One of those blurred red shapes in long johns, the one in war paint whose hand I'd creased, had found his gun. He stepped back into the flickery firelight and tried to use both hands, his mangled right and his pristine left, to train the gun on me.

I spun to face him and fired off three fast rounds.

They caught him in the leg, the knee, and of course, that previously pristine hand. I doubted he'd play piano again, if he ever had. He fell screaming.

Then I seemed to be the only one standing.

The six raiders were on the ground around me, their screams diminishing to whimpers, as they writhed in the dust like Indians who'd had a mite too much peyote.

The echoing gunfire, which had thundered in the night for what had seemed like forever but was probably a matter of seconds, had faded into silence. Only the rushing of the waterfall remained. Even the music box was silent. It sat there, not a nick in it, waiting to be returned to its owner.

Coop moved into view, with Annabelle following. She had a stunned expression.

"Are you . . . are you all right?" she managed. No Southern accent; sincere concern.

I nodded.

Then her face bunched up. " '*Ugly* Annie'?"

Coop said to her dryly, "You must admit, it was amusin'."

I said to him, "Was it you got that hatchet-faced character?"

Coop said nothing, thumbs looped in his gun belt.

Annabelle's eyes were large; she pointed at the good marshal. Her voice was a whisper, as if that would keep Coop, standing next to her, from hearing: "You should've seen *him* draw!"

I gave him a narrow-eyed stare. "Took your time answering my whistle."

"A man could've got killed out there," he said.

"Really?"

"It was your show." He shrugged. "Good to see you livin' up to your potential."

I shook my head. Surprisingly, I felt good—not even very winded. I'd had luck tonight; I hoped I hadn't used all of it up, before getting to that poker table in St. Louis.

"Coop," I said, "you're lucky I'm not dead."

"Oh?"

"If I was," I said, "I swear to God I'd kill you."

There was a long moment where he and I tried to decide whether we were mad at each other or grateful. Then Annabelle broke the silence.

"I'll look for the money," she said.

"I'll help," I said.

10

A Real Hero

Our six prisoners—and all six had survived last night's gunfight, none bleeding so bad that the bandages and poultices Coop and I whipped up couldn't curtail it—sat tied to each other and to the wheels of the scorched Conestoga wagons they'd not so long ago raided.

They'd had to sit there through the night, hurting, ropes tight around 'em, but the good Christian settler women had provided them with blankets and such, in addition to hellfire lectures about the evil they'd done.

The nearest law was in Crystal River. Getting these owlhoots—not to mention these poor pilgrims they'd waylaid—back to civilization seemed a job better handled by Coop than yours truly. I felt I'd done enough, and I had a poker game waiting.

But right now my biggest concern was breakfast. I rustled up some firewood, got the flames going and, speaking of rustling, started heating up some leftover stew I'd found at the outlaws' camp last night. Our long-johned guests had apparently helped themselves to a steer or two, in addition to welcoming wagon trains to the frontier.

Annabelle drifted over; she'd slept in one of the wagons, and her blonde hair was an attractive mess.

"Are you supposed to be the chef?"

"I might've asked you—you bein' a woman and all— but since we're a little short on provisions, I didn't want to risk you shrinkin' the food."

I was still in my frilly, formerly lucky shirt, after all.

"I know how to *cook*," she said, mildly indignant, even a little hurt.

"I'm sure. Famous Southern delicacies. But where are you gonna find chitterlings and collard greens out here?"

She eyed the black kettle I'd commandeered from our pioneer hosts suspiciously, and sniffed at its pungent aroma. "And what's that?"

"I really shouldn't say in front of a delicate prairie flower like yourself."

"That bad, huh?"

"No—it's sort of a rude name, is all. Rough cowboy talk."

She smirked. "I can take it, Maverick."

"I'm sure you can. It's called son-of-a-bitch stew."

She snorted a laugh. "Big deal. What's in it?"

"Calf brains, tongue, liver, heart, kidneys, and sweetbreads, mixed with a few wild vegetables. Very big among the cowhands."

I don't know whether you'd call her expression one of extreme distaste or abject horror. But it was one of those. Maybe both.

Coop came walking up; he'd been chatting with the settler women, over where they were tending their wounded men by the least-harmed wagon.

"Smells good!" he said. "What is that, son-of-a-bitch stew? Pardon my French, Mrs. Bransford."

Annabelle rolled her eyes and took a step away from the fire. She shuddered, once.

"You may be interested to know," Coop told me loftily, "those fine brave ladies, and their menfolk as well, have positively identified our prisoners as their raiders."

As if the money and music box we'd found weren't proof enough.

"No kidding," I said. To both of them, I said, "I told you there were no hostiles in this part of the country."

Coop frowned, shook his head. "One thing troubles me."

"What?"

"Those war drums we heard yesterday . . . we didn't imagine 'em. And that sure as hell weren't thunder. *Somebody* was pounding away on those skins."

We were facing each other, Coop and me, not paying any attention to Annabelle, who was standing away from the smell of my stew. When she spoke, it startled us.

"Maybe . . . maybe it was *them*."

Her voice was trembling, frightened, in a way I'd never heard before from this confident young woman.

But when I turned and saw her pointing, her eyes showing white all the way around, I understood.

They were mounted, and they were armed, and they were Indians.

No doubt about it: this was not white men fooling around, or passing the buck (so to speak). This was a full-fledged, feathers-and-tomahawks, mocassins-and-buckskins, bows-and-arrows war party.

"No hostiles in this part of the country?" Annabelle asked through her teeth.

I shrugged. "Maybe a few."

At least fifty, anyway, and they were lined up as if preparing to charge. Their silence was the worst part. It promised war whoops, savage screams, gunfire, cries of pain.

Right now it was just an awful, unceasing silence.

Then hoofbeats exploded the calm, a thundering but unshod sound, as if a thousand more savages on horseback were approaching, hell-bent for every white scalp left in these parts.

But it was only one.

Only one redskin rider on horseback, whom the others parted to accommodate, as he—on a powerful, white, rippling-muscled steed--took his rightful place in their midst. He was a massive figure, leaping to life straight from myth, his bare, war-painted chest roped with muscle, his oval face baked by the sun, streaked with war paint, and creased with cruelty, both his own, and that of the white men who'd invaded his homeland. He carried a tall, feather-and-scalp-decorated spear, and on a head held high was a magnificent red, white, and blue feathered headdress.

"I think that one's the chief," Annabelle offered.

"No. Really?" I said.

"You were an Indian scout," Coop said quietly. "Do you recognize their markings?"

I nodded gravely. "The Fakawi tribe." I shook my head. "I thought Screaming Eagle and his cutthroats had been chased to Mexico long ago."

The chief was guiding his horse toward us, the horizon behind him obscured by his men. As the white steed trotted forward at his behest, the chief's unsmiling gaze burned into us like a flaming arrow.

He stopped.

He spoke.

In the guttural language of the Fakawi, which I'd learned so long ago, his face impassive as stone, his voice as harsh as the barren land that once had been his domain and that of his noble kind, he intoned, "Maverick—I thought that was you. Did you come for the money I owe you?"

Actually, there is no word for "Maverick" in Fakawi; he called me Unbranded Cow, which is the closest they've got. So if you don't mind, when translating, I'll take the liberty of using "Maverick."

Anyway, keeping a grave expression going, I turned to Coop and Annabelle, as well as the pioneer women and men who were huddling together fearfully at the sight of these savages, and asked, "Anyone get that? Anyone speak Fakawi?"

Coop shook his head, no, and so did the others.

"I know a few words," I said.

"Bret," Annabelle said, touching my arm. "Be careful."

I touched her pretty face and nodded, bravely.

Then I walked up to Screaming Eagle (who called himself Joseph, now) and said, in Fakawi, "What's the war paint for?"

"Just out fooling around. It gets us away from the women."

"Ah. Don't smile. Promise me you won't smile."

"I never smile."

"Sure you do. That's one of your 'tells.' That's how I won the thousand you owe me. I want a favor."

"How long will it take? There's a breeze this morning, and it's cold without a shirt."

"I'll make it quick. Scream at me."

Joseph unleashed a bloodcurdling shriek that even scared me. I heard the settlers scurrying for cover, in panic. Coop moved up next to me and whispered.

"What's he saying?"

I took Coop by the arm and walked him near Annabelle, and the three of us huddled.

I said, "Seems we've committed a terrible sacrilege."

"No!" Annabelle said, her fingers flying to her lips.

"Yes. This is sacred ground."

"But we didn't know it was sacred!" she said. "Tell him. Tell him we didn't know it was sacred. Tell him we'll move on, right now!"

I thought about that, nodded.

Walked back over to Joseph and said, "Shake your war bonnet around, get those feathers goin', and fire your rifle in the air. Look mad. Babble at us. You know—a real Crazy Horse routine."

Joseph took his rifle from its beaded-cloth scabbard and fired it into the air, wildly, screaming obscenities in Fakawi. I won't provide an exact translation, but it was mostly about how undignified it was for a tribal chieftan to lose money playing poker to a white man.

I returned to Coop and Annabelle, shaking my head.

"Doesn't he understand we didn't know?" she said.

"He understands," I said. "He just doesn't care. He says . . . he says his gods demand a sacrifice."

"What kind of sacrifice?" Coop asked.

I couldn't say it.

"Spit it out, son!" Coop said.

I tasted my tongue; shook my head. Muttered quietly, "A human sacrifice."

Annabelle's eyes were wide while Coop's were hooded.

I turned and called to Joseph, in Fakawi, "You're doin' fine! Now, start pointing your finger at us, like you're bawling us out. And then, well, bawl us out. Don't yell. Just angry."

The brooding chieftan shook his finger at us; it was as if he was singling us out to pay for all the sins committed on his people by our kind. His words, in Fakawi, were actually a recipe for boiled dog and cherry paste, but (other than me) his audience didn't know that. Considering Annabelle's reaction to the ingredients of my stew, maybe that was for the better.

As I faced Coop and Annabelle, I had never looked more worried, not even facing three queens up in seven-card stud.

"If one of us can pass the Indian bravery ritual, then they won't kill the rest of us."

"What's the Indian bravery ritual?"

"They cut off both your hands," I said. "If you don't make a sound, you're no longer considered a white man—you're Fakawi."

Coop frowned. "Both hands?"

"Both hands. Not a happy prospect for a card player."

I walked over to Joseph and said, in his Fakawi, "Hold up one finger and holler some."

For a natural leader of men, Joseph wasn't a bad temporary follower: he raised a finger, whooped and howled, like a white man's worst nightmare. A bobcat foaming at the mouth would seem easier to tame.

I glanced back at them. "One of us has to go with him right now—or he'll slaughter the lot of us."

Suddenly Joseph burst out laughing. He couldn't stop for a moment. A silly laugh, at that.

I gave him a dirty look.

"Sorry, Maverick," he said, getting under control, "I just never had this much fun with white people before."

I turned back to Coop and Annabelle and worked up my somberest expression. "He's laughing, just thinking about the pain he's going to inflict. He loves to watch the white man suffer."

Annabelle shivered, stood close to Coop. "You can see he's sadistic," she said, "just *looking* at him."

Joseph fired his rifle in the sky, and shrieked.

"He wants blood *now*," I told them, and then said to Joseph in Fakawi, "Let's not get carried away, all right?"

"Who's your pretty friend?" Joseph asked, still in his native tongue, of course. "She's good looking, for a white girl."

That was a good idea. I tried not to grin.

"Point to her," I said to Joseph, "and I'll tell 'em you want her."

"I do want her. Is she yours? Trade you four horses."

"Tempting," I said in Fakawi. "Look her over. Don't hide your feelings. Then do one of those mating call whoops of yours."

He rode over to her, and smiled down at her; she backed away, grabbing onto me. Joseph looked lecherous as hell when he proposed marriage to her, in Fakawi, and it sounded much worse than just marriage.

"I notice you didn't tell her," I said to him in Fakawi, "that you got three wives already."

"I was working up to that," Joseph said testily.

"What did he say?" Annabelle asked, frightened, clinging to my arm.

I shook my head, no. It was too terrible for her ears. Instead I said, "I'll die before I let him touch you."

"But there's so many of them," she said. "How can you—"

"Don't show fear! It only inflames them." I turned to Coop. "We've got to end this before it gets out of hand. It's got to be one of us. I'd suggest turning over one of our prisoners, but I'm afraid Screaming Eagle wouldn't settle for damaged goods."

Coop nodded.

"Besides," I said nobly, "those men have to be brought to justice."

He put a hand on my shoulder. "You've done enough, Bret. I'll go."

"No. I can't allow—"

"I almost got you killed twice already."

"Testing my courage. That's why I'm ready for this. And I can't do *your* job—saving these women and children, getting the wounded settlers back to civilization, takin' that lawless rabble back to justice. No . . . a man's gotta do what a man's gotta do."

Annabelle, eyes wide and genuinely fluttery for once, said, "Did your pappy say that, Bret?"

Not hardly.

"He should have," I said. I turned to Joseph and called, in Fakawi, "Be with you in a minute!"

I gathered my things—most important, of course, was my saddlebag of money; I could almost hear that St. Louie riverboat ringing its bell—and Coop and Annabelle saw me off while Joseph waited patiently atop his steed, back in line with his braves.

Annabelle, truly emotional for once, even if I did have to fool her into it, threw herself into my arms, clinging to me. "Don't go, Bret . . . please don't go . . ."

"I like it when you call me 'Bret.' "

"Oh, Bret . . ."

"Listen to me now. Something very important. Vital."

She drew away just a touch, so she could gaze lovingly into my eyes. "What, Bret? My dear, dear Bret?"

"When you're going to bluff, don't flick your fingernail against your front teeth. That's the second dead giveaway you got to work on."

Her eyes began to well with tears. "You've changed so, Bret . . . at a time like this, to be thinkin' only of me . . ."

I touched her cheek with a gentle hand. "Fare thee well, Annabelle . . ."

I gave her a tiny kiss, but she clutched me, kissed me passionately. And since I didn't have any money in my pocket, and my saddlebag was snug, this time it was only me she was after.

Then I left her arms, and walked to the nearby Coop, who stood holding the reins of my horse. Coop gave me a manly embrace and I took the reins and walked Ollie toward Joseph and his fierce (looking) war party. Halfway there, I turned, put on a brave, trembling smile, and held up my arms, wiggling the fingers of both hands.

"It's all right," I said. "Don't cry. When they cut these off, my lucky shirt will fit again . . ."

Annabelle sobbed into Coop's shoulder.

Then I mounted my horse and rode off to join Joseph, while Coop comforted the heartsick Annabelle and the pioneers watched in awe as a real hero rode off to meet his fate at the hands of savages. It was a tale they would tell their children and their children's children. . . .

Riding at Joseph's side, I began to grin.

Joseph, speaking in the perfect English the missionaries taught him, said, "What was the point of all that?"

"Nothin', really," I said. "But I tell you one thing—I could die happy right now."

Then I turned my horse back to face the wagon train again, and pulled on the reins, and Ollie reared as I cast my compatriots a heroic wave, silhouetted against the sky.

11

Dangerous Frame

The Fakawi village showed few signs that its chief—who had assumed the name "Joseph" even among his tribe—was well versed in the white man's ways. Joseph's treks into the wilds of civilization were usually profitable, with the occasional exception, like the thousand he'd lost to me in San Francisco.

But I knew for a fact that he and Dandy Jim Buckley had together sold enough "Indian land" to citified suckers to constitute two Texas-sized territories.

The spoils of such crafty counterattacks on the white man, however, hadn't corrupted the culture of his little community, much. The conical elk-skin teepees, scattered along the stream bank, were much the same as they'd been before the Great White Father came along, though to the time-worn custom of keeping a fire going at the center of a teepee's circular interior had been added steel kettles. Here and there, among the villagers—men in their skin shirts, buckskin leggings, and moccasins; women in their deerskin dresses with laced cowhide leggings up to their knees—a bowler hat or a storebought moccasin provided a reminder of the white trader's influence. So did the occasional toy—a ball, a top, other such trinkets—which occupied the Fakawi children.

A more glaring example of the intrusion of the white man's ways was Joseph's latest toy, an up-to-date version of the velocipede, with a pedal on either side to propel it, and equal-sized steel wheels replacing the old wooden variety.

I was trying this newfangled boneshaker out, and even though it had pedals, Joseph walked along with me, helping me keep balance. The sun was high, and it was warm but not unpleasantly hot as I took in the vista of the Fakawi village, sunlight glittering off the stream.

"Beautiful here," I said.

"Too beautiful," Joseph said, guiding me along.

We were speaking in English, by the way.

"How can anyplace be *too* beautiful?" I asked.

"As my old father, the great Fakawi chieftain, once said: 'Marry an ugly woman, my son, and discourage the competition.' "

"Advice worthy of *my* pappy," I said, getting his meaning.

But Joseph's lecture had only just begun. "Next time your people drive us from our land, I'm going to search out a fine span of swampland where you'll leave us the hell alone. You will look here and not find us; you will look there and we will be as the wind. The white invader will raise his fist to the sky and shake it in frustration. He will look to the clouds and shout, 'Where the Fakawi? Where the Fakawi?' "

"How often I've asked myself that very question," I said.

A rhythmic, musical, deep-throated pounding attracted my attention. Down by the stream, some Fakawi braves were sitting with crossed legs, pounding on the tightly stretched buffalo skins of their ceremonially decorated war drums.

Distracted momentarily, I almost lost my balance, but Joseph steadied the machine.

"These beasts can be tricky," Joseph said. "They say they'll replace the horse, but I have my doubts."

"Well, they smell better than a horse," I said. "And you don't have to watch your step around 'em."

"Yes," Joseph said. "They don't eat. But they also don't reproduce."

"This isn't nature," I said, getting off, and letting Joseph take the thing. "It's commerce."

Joseph nodded solemnly and wheeled the bicycle over and rested it on the ground, near his teepee, which of course was the grandest in the village. Through the drawn-back flap of the teepee's slit opening, I could glimpse incredible animal skins covering the earthen floor and elaborate feather headdresses adorning the walls.

The drums continued their measured, resonant tattoo.

"What's that about?" I asked him.

"We had a bad harvest. Indian Affairs agent told me about a Russian archduke traveling through who wanted to see the *real* West . . . you know, 'cowboys and wild injuns.' "

"Aw," I said. "And you can fulfill half of the archduke's dreams."

Joseph nodded, seeming mildly disgusted with himself. "We make fools of ourselves, whooping around in this war paint, beating those stupid drums. Hadn't used them in years, you know—you should have seen the dust we raised when we first started in pounding on them."

"Is the money good?"

Again, Joseph nodded.

"Then don't worry about it," I said. "He's the mark, not you."

"He likes us to speak like *real* Indians. The ones in your cheap fiction. '*How*, white man . . . ugh'. . . ."

" 'Ugh' is right," I said.

He shook his head. "You people can be such jackasses."

A gloomy silence descended on the chief. Apparently the demeaning nature of the way he and his bucks lately were making a buck had got the best of him. He wandered away from me, stared out into the shimmering stream.

"Hey," I said. "So the guy's an idiot. You're conning *him*, remember?"

"That's not it, Maverick." He seemed genuinely miserable. "It's the thousand I owe you."

"What about it?"

"I don't have it."

"What about all this money you're making from the archduke?"

He gestured with widespread arms at his village. "It has gone into feeding and clothing my people. Winter is coming."

"How much of it *can* you pay back?"

"Would you accept wampum?"

I groaned and shook my head. Now I was the miserable one. "I don't think wampum'll buy me any chips in St. Louie."

"St. Louie?"

"Big poker championship—the biggest. I only got a couple days to rustle up three thousand for the entry fee."

"That's a fat entry fee, Maverick."

"It's a spit in the ocean, friend. The entry fee is twenty-five thousand."

The impassive mask of Joseph's face cracked, his eyes lighting up, a smile tickling his mouth. "You've got twenty-two thousand dollars?"

"That's right."

"In cash? I've never seen that much money in one place. Where is it? Can I see it? Can I touch it?"

"Hey, I'm your white blood brother, remember. No swindles, none of those close haircuts you boys used to specialize in—"

"None of that," he said. He was as excited as a little

kid at the prospect of running his hands through such a huge pile of Uncle Sam's greenbacks.

So I went over to Ollie, and reached in my saddlebag for the leather-drawstring money pouch. Joseph was hovering over my shoulder, eyes wide with Christmas-morning anticipation as I opened it up and found sheafs of cut-up seed catalogue pages.

It hit me like a physical blow. I took out the worthless bundles—they'd even been cut too small for decent privy use—and stared at them, trying to make them green. Then the wind took them, blowing them from my fingertips, scattering them across the village.

Annabelle.

"How could she steal from me," I said, "when I was riding off to face torture and possible death at the hands of savages?"

"A woman did this?"

"A woman. A no-good, rotten, lousy, double-crossing . . . hell. Well, as Pappy used to say, 'Man is the only animal you can skin twice.' "

"And your poker game in St. Louie?"

I watched as seed-catalogue "bills" blew across the landscape. "I'll never make it there, now . . . far as that game's concerned, I'm a dead man."

"A dead man," Joseph said, nodding, commiserating.

"Exactly," I said.

And now Joseph did something remarkable.

He smiled, a smile as sunny as the sunniest one I ever managed.

"A dead man," he said. "That may be a very profitable thing to be . . ."

* * *

A short ride from the beautiful landscape in and around the Fakawi village was the ravaged terrain of a burned-out forest. Joseph indicated this was the work of the archduke; a campfire got out of control, an unintentional but nevertheless severe sin committed against the Indian gods whose lands these were.

I was helping Joseph and his people get even, and with a little luck would start building myself a new stake; not enough for the St. Louis tournament, obviously, unless miracles awaited me.

But you have to start somewhere, and I was starting back on the path to fortune (by both its definitions) in a burned-out forest, wearing the buckskins, moccasins, and war paint of a Fakawi brave. I'd also had my pale skin darkened by berries, and from a distance—even fairly close up, actually—I could easily pass for an "injun."

On the way here, we'd had a hilltop view of the archduke's camp, sprawling luxuriously across a meadow. Tents surrounded a mammoth prairie schooner, the interior of which Joseph had described in detail: elaborate framed paintings of Russian tableaus, plush furnishings, silver tea services. You know—roughing it.

Back in the village, Joseph had explained, "He's bored with killing bobcats and deer. I think 'The Mighty One from Across Big Water' is ready for bigger game."

"Bigger game?"

Joseph nodded. " 'Injun.' "

And that "injun" was me.

As the hoofbeats of their horses approached, I dou-

bled over in apparent pain, groaning, my face hidden.
Their voices came clearly to me over the scorched landscape.

"I'm having second thoughts," intoned a regal, Rus-
sian-tinged, yet reed-thin voice. "This can't possibly
be legal."

Joseph, doing his best pidgin "injun," said, "If no
one find out, legal as killing elk. Beside—white man
been doing this for years."

The thin voice was tremulous with anticipation. "I've
killed animals on every continent, more species than
you people have beads and blankets . . . but I've never
hunted game *this* big before."

Joseph grunted, then said, "Need much wampum for
hunt like this."

"How much?"

I didn't hear Joseph's reply; maybe he was holding up
a certain number of fingers.

"We're not going to tie him up, are we?" the archduke asked. "Somehow that wouldn't seem . . . sporting."

The archduke was a real prince.

"Him loose. See? Dying, anyway. Him have much
pain. Put him out of misery."

I could hear Joseph and the duke dismounting.
Glancing up, I watched the fleshy, mustached aristo-
crat—dressed more as if for a fox hunt, than a man out
to bag human prey—lumber toward me, a huge, single-
shot Sharps rifle in his hands. Joseph was carrying a
bow almost as tall as the archduke.

The Fakawi chief held up a halting hand. "White

man stay here. Indian rites say, me go now, give dying warrior courage."

The archduke nodded, rifle at the ready as he stood, nervously shifting from one foot to the other, as Joseph approached me.

We spoke in Fakawi.

"There's a blank in that gun," I asked, "like you said?"

"Couldn't get to it," Joseph said. "He never let it out of his hands."

"Then forget it," I said. "I'm not risking my life for a measily couple hundred."

"I got him up to five hundred."

I thought about it. The ways things were going, it might be worth the risk.

"Stand clear!" the archduke shouted. "Tell him to start running! I don't want to lose the light."

Joseph stood in the line of fire, arms outstretched. "No! No . . . is wrong."

The archduke lowered the huge Sharps in confusion, as Joseph trotted over to him.

The chief waggled a scolding finger, giving his patron a stern look. "Injun shot by white-man weapon never reach Happy Hunting Ground."

"How do you expect—"

"Injun must die way of noble savage . . . here."

And he handed the archduke the enormous bow, and drew an arrow from his beaded buckskin quiver.

Like a whiny child, the archduke complained, "But I don't know how to *use* one of these . . ."

"Ugh. Is easy."

"All right, then," the archduke said impatiently,

hefting the bow, positioning an arrow. "Tell him to start running."

Joseph turned to me and, in Fakawi, said, "Don't go too fast. You're supposed to be dying, remember."

"Are you kidding?"

"If you can't trust a blood brother, who can you trust?"

"Ugh," I said.

And I ran, but sort of limping, weaving, not trying to present too easy a target as the archduke raised the tremendous bow and took aim.

I ducked behind a tree and heard his arrow *thud* into it, where it shuddered almost as much as I did, hearing the splintering sound.

But there was another, almost simultaneous sound: the archduke howling in pain.

Peeking around the tree, I could see that the archduke had dropped the bow, and was bent over, shaking both his hands if they were on fire and he was trying to put it out. That hefty bow must have made his hands sting mighty bad.

I stayed ducked behind the tree while their voices sailed across the mostly burned-away landscape.

"Give me my rifle!" the archduke was sputtering.

"More wampum."

"How much?"

Again, Joseph must have held up fingers; the exact amount, I couldn't hear.

"What about denying this brave the Happy Hunting Ground?" the archduke asked.

"Never like him much anyway," Joseph said. "Shoot quick."

I started running again, feeling confident Joseph had rigged up the Sharps with a blank load—if you couldn't trust a blood brother, who could you trust?

The burnt trees shook with the report of the big gun, and one of them blew apart, taking the blast intended for me. Nonetheless, I fell to the earth, screaming with pain, clutching my chest, squeezing my fist over the pouch of deer blood. The archduke was such a crack shot, he'd managed to shoot me in the back and yet get me in the front—right in the heart.

Joseph's moccasined feet rustled leaves as he ran up to me, turned me over with a foot, and said, "Ugh. Him plenty dead."

The archduke's voice was trembling with excitement. "Are you sure?"

"Mighty One want scalp?"

"No! But I would . . . would like to do this *again*. Tomorrow possibly?"

"No. Rest of tribe healthy. Come back in winter."

I could hear them mount their horses, though before they rode off, that good sport the archduke said, "Doesn't seem right to just leave him for the vultures."

"Him like. That his name."

"What do you mean?"

"Running Vulture," Joseph said. "He wait now for feathered friends."

It was dusk when I bent by the stream to wash off my war paint. The Indian drums were silent. Here and there, orange blurs of campfires dotted the Fakawi village.

Joseph came riding in and hopped off his horse.

"That fool could have killed me!" I said. "That was no blank round, my fine 'feathered friend'—"

The chief grinned as he handed me his huge bow from over his shoulder. "Here—you try it."

Shrugging, I took an arrow and aimed for a tree across the stream. The pull was brutal, and the rough wood scraped my hands; the arrow went sailing crazily, plopping into the water, while I dropped the bow and howled.

"After 'Mighty One from Across Big Water' used *that*," Joseph chuckled, "he couldn't hit a buffalo at two paces with that Sharps."

I knelt and dipped my burning hands into the stream. "What if he'd wanted to scalp me, like you offered?"

"Ugh," Joseph said. "That cost plenty more wampum."

I stood, as another thought dawned. "You know, one of these days I'm gonna run into my stagecoach companions, and have to explain how I got away from you ferocious savages."

He shrugged. "Tell 'em you got us likkered up on firewater, and slipped away in the confusion."

"Think they'll believe that?"

He put a hand on my shoulder and solemnly intoned, "Maverick, if today taught you nothing else, you should have learned one thing: as my father, the great chief, used to say, white people will believe anything."

Good point.

"Anyway," he said, and dug some greenbacks out of his buckskins, "I can pay you that thousand I owe you, now."

"I appreciate that," I said, sincerely. Since I hadn't

heard the negotiation, Joseph could have kept it at five hundred. On the other hand, knowing Joseph, he probably wormed two grand out of the archduke.

Joseph slipped an arm around my shoulders. "After all, if you can't trust a blood brother—"

"This is *nine* hundred," I said.

12

Hell's Waiting Room

I had decided to press on to St. Louis, anyway.

Problem was, all the money I had was that thousand dollars from Joseph, and another near-thousand Annabelle hadn't got to—my poker winnings from Crystal River.

But Annabelle might just be foolish enough to use the money I'd raised to enter the competition herself; if so—and if I could reach our mutual destination before she paid the fee—I would politely request of Mrs. Bransford that she kindly fork my dough back the hell over before I shook it out of her.

Crossing the stream, I moved up onto the rutted

stagecoach road that would keep me going in the right direction, as well as provide me with the occasional way station for good, drink, and rest. I could still make it. Make it easily.

The morning was warm, but not hot, and Ollie and I kept up a steady, but not torturous, pace, riding the level space between the ruts. The land had turned desolate again, a boulder-strewn flat that the road wound through lazily, and as we came around a bend, a riderless horse wandered our way, its reins loose and hanging.

I slowed, but kept moving, looking to see if a rider had been thrown.

And there he was, along the roadside, face-down against some rocks where he seemed to have landed, whether thrown or fallen. He wore the weathered, trail-dusty clothes of a cowhand or drifter, and he was moaning, almost whimpering.

He looked to be hurt, maybe bad. His body was twisted at an unnatural angle. Maybe his legs were broke, both of them.

I reined in, hopped down off Ollie.

"Hang on, friend!" I called.

His only response was to groan louder. Walking Ollie over, I bent over the poor varmint and, gently, turned him on his back. The face that looked up at me wouldn't have been pleasant even if he wasn't in pain: stubble-faced, leathery-skinned, he had one eye that went north and another that went west.

I didn't hardly know which one to look in.

He whispered something. I leaned closer.

"Sucker," he said.

They had crept up behind me and one of them had my gun before I could even turn around. Somebody else kicked me in the side of the head, and the world went swimming as I tumbled to the ground.

I wasn't unconscious, just stunned and in a world of pain. Two men were hovering over me—one of them had a rope-burned neck, and the other was an old friend.

Of sorts.

A buzzard in a black sombrero and demilitarized cavalry jacket, with a black scruffy beard.

A buzzard name of Angel.

Who, just as I was getting on my feet, kicked me in the stomach. I gagged and retched, and then he kicked me there again. Harder. Couldn't breathe now. Gasped for air, but didn't seem to do no good.

I was rolling on the ground, hugging my stomach, probably turning white as sugar. Sour bile came up in my throat, and I heard Angel's nasty, gloating voice.

"You should have paid them cowhands more, Maverick," Angel was saying. "They got to drinkin' and boastin' and started laughin' at me. Told me you *paid* 'em to fall down. You know what? For me, they fell down for free."

The man I'd tried to help, the one with the wandering eyes, was going through my pockets; they found Joseph's thousand, and the Crystal River poker winnings. The hundred pinned in my shirt, however, was still mine.

Not that I could see it doing me any good right now, or for that matter, in the future, since I didn't seem to have much of one.

"I'd never let you make that poker game, nohow," Angel was saying, as his two sidekicks kicked and slammed fists into me, "but I mighta let you live. Then you went and done made a fool of me."

He joined in on the beating, which was the most vicious I've ever had, and I've had a few. I tried to fight back, but it was like a kitten pawing the air: the attack had been too sudden, too savage. It was all I could do to stay conscious.

"Enough!" Angel said, after what seemed a mighty long while. "Let's find a cottonwood to decorate. . . ."

Which brings us back to a stormy, thunder-rolling sky and a handsome devil—me—with his hands tied and his neck in a noose, sitting atop a horse who was surprisingly well-behaved, considering he'd only been under me a few days and there was a sack of rattle-snakes at our mutual feet.

Actually, at this point, the noose wasn't on my neck anymore; I had managed to work it up under my nose without spooking Ollie. The slithering snakes ought to do that soon enough, but for the moment, the horse hadn't noticed, or just plain wasn't impressed by a dozen or so whopping rattlers, who could have gone off in any direction at all, but chose to slide and slink toward us.

A thunderclap shook the sky and the earth, this tree included; in a day turned dark by the storm, lightning threw its momentary silvery light on the world—a world where a dozen or so rattlers were now curling and raising up and shaking their behinds, noisily.

Now Ollie noticed them, or at least that was how I took the way he raised up his head, but at least he stayed planted on all fours.

"Easy boy," I soothed, trying to work that noose up over my nose. It wasn't that big a nose. It shouldn't be that hard to—

And Ollie bolted.

He was gone, charging off, barely disturbing the snakes, and I was hanging, swaying, hands behind me, rattlers below.

My neck hadn't snapped because the noose was no longer around it; the rope burned my upper lip, caught under my nose as it was, and the discomfort was incredible—as if some giant creature were trying to pull my head off like the cork from a stubborn wine bottle.

Despite the pain, I was tired. Could I die hanging like this? Did I really want to drop into that writhing nest of rattlers? Would the pain eventually ebb, and perhaps the rattlers give up, and crawl away? These and hundreds of other awful, frantic thoughts flickered through my mind like the ever-flashing lightning, as my energy ebbed and my struggling became more feeble and, finally, I just hung there motionessly.

I always said luck was the lady that I loved the best, but truth be told, I never depended on her, never called on her. I memorized the tables and I played the percentages. I took the advice Pappy told Bart and me when we left the ranch in Texas: "Never hold a kicker—never draw to an inside straight."

I closed my eyes. It wasn't a prayer, exactly. But if ever Lady Luck were going to show up and bail me out of a losing game, now was the time.

A deafening explosion shook the tree and my ears—another thunderclap?—and the whole damn branch I was hanging from got ripped from the tree. *Lightning?* I hadn't seen it strike, but damnation, I was falling!

Then I was landing, hard, hitting the ground and scattering the snakes.

For a moment.

Then there I was, eyes open, on my side, breath knocked out of me, hands tied behind me, and every rattler on God's green earth slithering toward me, smiling their awful Satan's smiles.

They were poised there, the monsters, as if preparing to take a vote on who would bite me first.

So much for Lady Luck.

Then I sensed her. Not Lady Luck, not hardly, but somebody, a woman, a little old woman in strange, mismatching, ill-fitting, patchwork garments. She had the burlap sack in her gnarled hands and billy bejiggered if she wasn't wandering around amongst the snakes, calm as a reverend passing the plate, plucking them from the ground and putting 'em in the sack.

They didn't even rattle when she would picked 'em up; in fact, they'd *stop* rattling.

It was the damnedest thing I ever saw. Also, the most wonderful—this peculiar little old gal, no bigger than a child, skirts rustling, scooping up rattlers like she was picking flowers in a garden.

And resting against the tree where she set it, trailing smoke out of its enormous barrel, was the biggest damn buffalo gun I ever saw.

That had been the thunder *and* the lightning that cut me down.

She tied the sack shut, like the writhing bag was a purse she was carrying, put it down over by the tree, and picked the buffalo gun back up. Her face was pinched, her eyes tiny and hard, but I didn't see cruelty there; she seemed a cross between a witch and a leprechaun, only instead of a broom, she had that blunderbuss, and instead of a pot of gold, she had a sackful of rattlers.

She trundled over to me and as I was about to say, "Thanks," she kicked me in the side. I flopped over on my back and said, "Ow!" Not eloquent, maybe, but to the point.

Then that buffalo gun was pointing right at my heart, and she was looming over me like the conscience I never quite had.

In a grave, gravelly voice, she said, "I aim to kill you, boy."

At this point, I was past being able to feel upset, or even scared. Mostly the concept of her killing me— now, after her cutting me down with that big gun and removing the threat of the rattlers—just seemed strange. Weird.

Of course, she seemed a mite weird herself.

Nonetheless, I had to ask: "Then why didn't you just leave me here, to hang?"

She moved the blunderbuss closer; the cuplike opening of the big gun barrel was against my chest. Her scowling old-woman/little-girl face would have been comical, perhaps, in other circumstances.

" 'Cause then you wouldn't have understood the gravity of your misdeed."

"My . . . misdeed? What misdeed? Who *are* you?"

"I'm nobody—nobody a'tall. Never you mind who I am! That don't matter a whit—what matters is you're a durn kidnapper."

"Kidnapper?"

"How dare you ask who I am? I'll tell you who I am—I'm your judge, jury, and executioner. Your misdeed, your crime, the crime you're gonna die for, the crime that's gonna condemn you to hell and damnation for all eternity and then some, is what you done to my friends."

"Your friends? *What* friends?"

That well and truly ticked her off; her eyes opened wide and her lips peeled back and out of that tiny frame came a huge roar: *"You kidnapped my rattlesnakes!"*

I knew I was in bad shape: I'd been beaten with an inch of my life, probably more like a half-inch, I'd just been hanged, then spent some memorable moments rolling around amidst rattlesnakes. But this was the first I realized I'd gone mad.

This was obviously a hallucination, and I was either in a fever or Hell's waiting room.

"Lady," I managed, "do I look like a rattlesnake rustler to you?"

She moved the gun back, just a touch, so she could look me over; she hadn't bothered before. When she was done, she said, "You got rattlesnake thief writ all over ya."

"You're wrong. I play cards. Poker."

She blinked. "In *that* shirt?"

And I started to laugh.

I just closed my eyes and laughed, but not for very long, because I couldn't find the strength to. I felt my body began to shake, uncontrollably, and my last thought, before blackness descended, was that maybe I'd been bit by a rattler, after all.

13

Lady Luck

A surprising thing happened.

I opened my eyes.

Was this heaven? As my vision came into focus, I could see pastoral vistas, in the form of beautifully framed oil paintings. I was nestled in a homemade quilt, delicately stitched, luxuriously downy. And on the floor was a vast, obviously expensive oriental carpet.

But I was on a cot that wasn't particularly comfortable, and the furnishings of this rustic, though expansive room were as mismatched as the clothing that little old woman had worn, everything from rough-hewn pioneer craft to the precision work of Victorian artisans.

And there were knickknacks everywhere—little collections, apparently, of this and that: colorful candles, rows of old bottles, grinning rag dolls, jars of buttons, stopped clocks (had Ugly Annie Bransford ridden through these parts?), hair combs, spittle cups, delicate figurines finely rendered by the hand of man, quartz-rock crystals formed by a more omnipotent craftsman. Slung in one corner were several bulging burlap sacks stuffed with God knew what, and, best of all, on the floor, slithering here and there as if they owned the place, were my old pals the rattlesnakes.

"Is this Hell?" I asked no one, sitting up on one elbow.

"No, ya durn fool," a gravel voice answered, "it's home—*my* home—and I'll mind ye not be so critical of a benevolent providence."

I sat up without putting my feet on the floor, as those snakes were sliding and gliding around down there.

My strange, wizened hostess was sitting, smoking a corncob pipe, rocking in a rocking chair three times her size. Her hodgepodge mismatched apparel was different than before, though her sense of style remained constant.

"You . . . you didn't kill me."

"Ain't you the keen-eyed cuss." She shook her head, chomped on her pipe. "Naw. You're too blamed dumb to steal my babies. It were them travelers what stopped at Gap Station, when I was over buyin' provisions."

"You take your . . . 'babies' along, when you go grocery shopping?"

She frowned. "It'd be cruel to keep 'em penned in,

don't ya think? Durn fool. You liked to die of fever, you know."

"Did a snake bite me?"

"No! You was almost hung!"

I rubbed my neck. "I remember."

"Plus which, you'd been abused by far worse creatures than my children. Never seen a man so bruised up and battered. Humans is a ruthless species, don't you think? Henry! Git down from there!"

I followed the eyes in her stern face to the corner of my cot where a rattler had slithered up the quilt; like a well-trained dog obeying its master, "Henry" dropped off the edge, onto the floor, and joined his brothers and sisters.

I touched fingertips to my forehead; my head seemed about to crack in two. "What . . . what day is this?"

She snorted, rocking, rocking. "Son, keepin' track of time lost its charm for me many a year ago."

"Well, how long have I been here?"

"More'n a day. Less'n a week." Suddenly, she scowled. "What are you lookin' at?"

"Say again?"

"You were lookin' at my blue bottles. Thinkin' about stealin' 'em—don't bother denyin' it. Ain't a blue bottle collection the like of it this side of London, England."

"I'm sure. I'm not going to steal your blue bottle collection."

"Go and ahead and try . . . my babies'll fang you to death, of course, but you're welcome to give 'er a try."

"No thanks."

She was calm again, rocking gently, smoke curling from the corncob. "Gettin' almost hunged, and havin'

the tar whaled out of ya, can put a feller off his feed.
You rest a spell. You'll be fine."

The creaking of her rocker on the wooden floor was
strangely soothing.

"Fine," she repeated. "You'll be fine . . ."

And I drifted off.

I sat in a wooden chair too small for me, at a wooden
table too small for me, a plush hand-sewn comforter
thrown around my shoulders. She had walked me over
here, the snakes parting for us like a wriggling Red
Sea. They were moving around down there, as I sat at
the table—sometimes one crawled across my boot.

For some reason, though, I'd stopped being afraid. I
didn't think these "children" would misbehave in front
of their mother.

She'd been cooking at a big black potbellied stove in
a corner of the room that was her kitchen, the hanging
pots, pans, kettles, and utensils making it look like she
regularly cooked for a regiment. But it seemed to be
only her and her babies.

She brought me a steaming plate of food, placing it
before me proudly; it looked like son-of-a-bitch stew,
and its aroma was spicy and not unpleasant, though
definitely unfamiliar. In the brown gravy, whiteish
chunks of meat floated.

"This isn't rattler, is it?" I asked.

"No!" she said, sitting down across from me with her
own steaming plate of stew. "I ain't a damn cannibal."

I took one bite. It wasn't bad, but my stomach was
queasy already, and the strangeness of the seasonings—

and the mystery of its contents—were less than appetizing.

"Clean your plate," she said. "You wanna git your strength back, don't ye?"

"What, uh . . . do you call this?"

"Sometimes it don't pay to ask too many questions. Let's just say it's a specialty of the house, and leave 'er at that."

"I'm not really hungry."

She looked down at the floor; her expression was cross. "What do you think?"

"Pardon?"

She exploded at me; it was like somebody opened a furnace: "I'm *not* talkin' to *you!*" Then she returned her gaze to the floor and, in a normal tone, said, "What's your opinion, Henry?"

A faint rattle was the response.

"You do? That's interestin'." She ate a bite of her food, then another, then said, "Henry thinks you oughta be punished. Henry thinks people what are rude and insultin' to a gracious hostess like yours truly *deserves* punishment."

I took a bite of food.

But she wasn't finished: "Did you kill the meat for that stew? No. Did you grow the vegetables for that stew? No. Did you know I worked hard to prepare it? Yes. Did you know I considered it a specialty of mine? Yes."

I took another bite.

"Now, as your hostess, it's my job to make you feel at home, make you feel comfortable, which me and my babies has gone way the hell around the bend to accomplish. So it's your job, as a guest, to make me feel 'preciated. You work on that, son."

I took another bite, and gave her the sunny smile.

"Yummy," I said.

That made her laugh. She laughed a good long while, finally winding down to say, "Now, that was a ripsnorter!"

Then she leaned across the little table and gave me a whap on the ear, like I was a misbehaving child.

"Life is serious!"

So I ate her mysterious specialty. She was right—I'd been rude. But it wasn't the strange stew, or even the rattlers on the floor that had "thrown me off my feed." It was more than just my strength I needed to get back—it was something else. Something inside me that had always moved me forward: the sense that there wasn't a game I couldn't win.

Bret Maverick could out-talk, out-smart, and, if absolutely necessary, out-shoot the best of them.

But right now I couldn't see my way past this hermit gal's cabin and her floorful of snakes.

She saw it, or sensed it, or something. Anyway, her harsh-sounding voice turned suddenly soft, even comforting. "You need your strength, son. Eat up."

"I don't know what I need my strength for, ma'am," I admitted. "My goal in life just got yanked out from under me."

"Your goal?"

I told her about the poker championship in St. Louis. Told her about the twenty-five-thousand-dollar entry fee, told her how I'd played poker practically all my life, how it was all I'd ever done, and how I wanted to know, for once and for all, if I really was the best at it there was.

"Never had a job but card-playin', son?"

"Not unless I couldn't avoid it. Like my ole pappy said, 'Work is all right for killin' time, but it's a shaky way to make a livin'.' ".

That made her smile, but she didn't whap me on the ear, this time. Instead, she said, "Lot of money at stake in this here game?"

I nodded. "But even if I could get there on time, I don't have the entry fee. I was a few thousand shy, anyway. And what I did have was stolen, and by now it's probably been spent."

She leaned forward, and her eyes were sharp as needles. "Lemme tell you somethin', son—there ain't nothin' more worthless on the face of this here earth than money."

"It wasn't the money."

"What was it then?"

"It was the knowing. Knowing I was the best."

She nodded. Then she grinned, and it was a crooked, yellow, but thoroughly charming grin. "Cleaned your plate, I see. Seconds?"

I managed a smile, pushed the wooden plate toward her. "Just a dab. I'm full, but it's too delicious to resist."

She really smiled, now, and glanced down at the floor. "See, Henry? You were wrong, and I was right— he *is* a nice boy."

So I ate her food, paid rapt attention to her babbling, and slept on her cot, slept soundly considering the slithery company I was keeping, and by late morning of the next day, I was starting to feel like myself again.

I sat in one of two wooden chairs she'd positioned by a large tree stump, while her "babies" sunned themselves nearby. For a day this warm, this bright, this sunny, there was an unusual number of rolling clouds, huge and white, moving across the horizon, almost racing, like runaway horses. Now and then there was an unmistakable growl of thunder, a threat of a storm at odds with the shining sun.

Over breakfast—a surprisingly conventional (and good) bacon, eggs, and potatoes—I had told her I'd be going, soon. I thanked her for her hospitality, and I gave her the only thing I had left: the hundred-dollar bill pinned inside my shirt.

"I'm sorry it's not more," I said.

She sat staring at the bill a long time. She didn't say you're welcome, and I couldn't even say if she was pleased.

Now, she came lumbering out of the cabin, two of her burlap "treasure bags" (as I'd learned she called them) slung over her shoulder. She looked like Santa's most pitiful elf. She trundled over and plopped the bags on the ground, and the sound of metal rattling against itself stirred the snakes, momentarily.

Nice to have a rattle unnerve *them*, for a change.

Her treasure bags contained the "loot" she'd come across in the last forty years. "Rough country hereabouts," she'd explained. "When I come 'pon a corpse, I help myself to their valuables. They's done with 'em, after all."

I hadn't argued. Why she'd hauled some of her swag

out by this tree stump was a bigger mystery than her stew.

"Been thinkin' about your financial sit-si-a-tion," she said. Smiling, tickled with herself, she pointed her corncob pipe at one of the burlap bags. "Guess what's in thar?"

"Supper?"

"There you go—bein' funny again. Want another smack?"

"No. Sorry. What's in 'thar'?"

"Just the answer to all your troubles."

Maybe she *was* one of Santa's elves, or a leprechaun.

I watched as she untied the mouth of the burlap bag and shook its contents out on the grass, sending rattlers scurrying for new sunning spots. The swag she was, apparently, ready to share with me ran to tin cups, tin plates, ladles, mugs, a few battered tin dishes.

"Some of them's real old . . . Revolutionary days . . . anty-cues, they call 'em."

"That's very kind, but, uh . . . I don't think the Commodore would accept an entry fee of . . . even the most valuable anty-cues."

"Who's the Commodore?"

"He runs the show. He's putting on the championship."

"Aw." Then she looked over at her sunning babies. "Maybe you was right, Henry. Maybe he's *not* such a nice boy."

"What did I do now?"

It was me answering, incidentally, not Henry.

She shook her head, and one gnarled finger. "I'm your elder, ain't I? Well, you should help your elders.

And when I say a word wrong, you oughter point it out, politely. It ain't anty-cues at all, is it?"

"Actually, I think it's pronounced 'antiques.' "

She whapped me on the ear. "Don't correct your elders! Now, if these anty-cues don't do the trick, maybe this privy paper *might*."

She opened the second sack, peeked in, smirked in disgust and disappointment, then held it so I could see its contents: green money.

Lots of it.

Stuffed like raked-up fall leaves in the sack, and just as crisp as fall leaves, only green. Green. So very green . . .

"Why, you have such a lovely smile," she said. "You should show it more often. Are you pleased? How much will you need?"

"Well . . . I . . . uh . . ."

"I done some cipherin'." She reached a hand inside and found a bundle already tied up with string. "Here's your entrance fee, and a little more, so you can buy some new duds. You're like to pop the buttons on that fancy little shirt."

"I don't know what to say." But just the same, I reached out my hand for the bundle of cash.

She pulled the bills back. "Now, I ain't no fool. I want somethin' in return."

"What? I'm afraid I don't have anything to offer—except more money, if I win."

"*When* you win! And I don't want more money, don't need more money. I got twenty-five times twenty-five thousand in this here sack."

"I'm afraid I don't have anything—"

Her eyes were bright and shining in the shriveled face. "You have somethin' few people have. Some calls it magic. Some calls it witchcraft, as I know all too well. You gambler fellas call it 'luck.' "

"I'm a percentage player, ma'am. I don't depend on luck."

"You don't have to *depend* on it. But you can still call on it . . . iffen it's in you." Her eyes narrowed as she sought the words to explain. "When I was little . . . I wasn't always a big, strappin' gal like this, y'know . . . animals used to foller me around. Not dogs or cats, any damn fool can attract them domesticated ninnies. No, I had butterflies and bees follerin' me . . . frogs and snakes and, anyhow, people thought I was magical, or mebbe a witch. Me, I never thought of it as magic—I just treated every one of God's creatures nice and cordial, and they responded in kind. You understand, son?"

"No."

"I didn't know that a body wasn't supposed to be able to communicate with such critters, so I went right ahead and did it, anyway. We got all sorts of things hid within us, boy. Special things. Magic things. Some calls it talents."

"I always had a way with cards," I admitted.

"I know. That's why I want you to do me that trick you done for your mother."

That startled me.

"How do you know about that? That's personal . . ."

Maybe the little biddy *was* a witch.

"You had fever, son. Babbled in your sleep. I listened." She shrugged. "It's my cabin—I'll listen, iffen I care to. Anyways, you *owe* me!"

I sighed. I did owe her—even if she rescinded her gift of bundled cash, I owed her my life. I nodded.

Now her voice was surprisingly gentle. "What's so personal about it?"

And then, suddenly, I was telling her things. Things I'd never spoken to any living soul about—assuming this little creature was a living soul.

"My mother was dying," I said. "And I wanted to give her something, before she left me. You'd think I could've had some magic, just a little luck, that day . . . but I didn't."

"Your mama liked card tricks?"

I smiled a little, nodded. "She was such a beautiful lady. A faro dealer—from Natchez to New Orleans, wasn't a finer one. She and Pappy met on a Mississippi riverboat. There was a big game, big as this one coming up in St. Louie. He won a ranch."

"A whole ranch?"

"A whole ranch. In Texas. He and my mother moved there, and Pappy put poker on hold for a while, and Ma retired from the tables, and together they raised a whole lot of cattle and two boys."

"You have a brother?"

"Bart. Year younger. We *both* of us always had a way with cards, even when we were little. Pappy encouraged it, and our mother didn't mind. She seemed to like it when I'd do card tricks. When I'd say, 'Pick a card,' she'd always pick the ace of spades."

The little old gal was sitting in the chair next to me, listening intently. The snakes started to stir at one point, and she raised a hand and they went still as stones.

"She was so awful sick," I said. "Lookin' so pale, there in bed. It's the only time I saw my pappy cry. She didn't cry, though. She called me, and Bart, over and touched our faces. I wanted to make her feel good, but . . . not with a trick. Not this time. So I said, 'You want to see the ace of spades, Mama?' And she said, 'Yes, dear, please,' and I gave her the cards, and she shuffled them, and I cut 'em . . . but I got it wrong. Oh, it was a spade, all right. A lousy nine. So much for magic. Or luck. Never trusted it again, no matter what you care to call it."

She reached into a pocket, somewhere, and a deck appeared in her hands.

"You do that for *me*," she said, then nodded at the bundled wad of bills in her lap, "and this here money is your'n."

"Do what for you?"

"Cut me the ace of spades! What else?"

"No. I can't do that."

"Why?"

"When I got older, come to find out the ace of spades is a death card. Can you imagine? My mama on her death bed, and I try to cut her the ace of spades . . ."

"But you didn't."

"No. I failed her."

"You're just full of ways you let her down, ain't you? First, you don't cut her the right card, then it turns out you picked the wrong card in the first place . . . you cain't do nothin' right, can you, son?"

I didn't say anything.

"Well, this time you're cuttin' the ace of spades, for me. And it don't mean death—it's just a card. But it's the card I want you to cut."

"The odds are fifty-one to one against."

"You could cheat. I seen how you handle them things."

"I don't cheat."

"I know. Cut the ace."

"No," I said testily. "Keep your money. The odds are too long . . . and I'm not failing again, not that way."

She snapped her fingers.

The rattlers seemed to gather around me; I'd become the center of their attention, their tails shaking, rattling, as they lived up to their name.

"You wouldn't," I said to her.

"In a fingersnap, when I'm riled."

And the rattlers were going wild.

I swallowed. "Maybe I will give it a shot," I said, "at that."

She snapped her fingers again, and the snakes calmed, slithered back into the sunshine, soaking it up.

"Figured you'd see the light," she said, and she got up from her chair and used the tree trunk as our table, where she shuffled the cards. She placed the wad of bills on the stump, next to the deck, as if this were the bet she were placing.

In a way, it was.

I took a deep breath, and concentrated; her eyes were on me—I could feel them—and I think even those damn snakes were watching. The wind came up, whispering encouragement, and my hand was poised over the deck. I felt a tingling. What was it? Luck? Magic? Witchcraft?

But then it was gone.

"I can't," I said. "Don't you understand? It would be like lettin' her down *again* . . ."

"They whipped you and beat you, t'other day, didn't they, son? Well, they . . . a diff'rnt 'they,' but a 'they' all the same . . . beat *me*, too, whipped me like a dog, an' left me to die."

"Why?"

" 'Cause I was little. Diff'rnt. Strange. They beat me and whipped me and I coulda just lay there and die, but somethin' inside o' me said, 'Fight back.' "

"Fight back? You became a hermit!"

She nodded and grinned, biting down on her pipe, beaming with pride. "Yup—best damn hermit there ever was, too!"

I looked at the deck; thought about the odds: 51 to one.

"I took my *own* path, son—and it's my preference to spend my time with my babies, 'cause they're not like people: they're direct, and they're honest. But my way ain't your way."

"My mother . . ."

"Loved you, and was proud of you, and land sakes, boy—she was dyin'! She didn't care a diddly-damn whether you cut 'er an ace or not! She cared that you were at her side. That you loved her."

"I did."

"Have you made your pappy proud?"

"He wouldn't admit it."

"But have you?"

"I think so."

"Well, then you can bet your ma feels the same way.
Cut the cards. Cut me an ace, boy!"

The wind came up, and I concentrated; closed my
eyes. Could I will myself an ace? I blotted out everything but the deck of cards, those 52 cards, faces
and numbers, hearts and diamonds and clubs and
spades. . . .

I cut the cards.

"Pick it up," I said, nodding to the cards, and then
I waited.

"It's a black ace!" she said giddily.

Exhilaration rushed through me; I opened my eyes.

She was holding up the ace of clubs.

"Real close, son! Real close."

"Hell," I said.

She shoved the bundle of cash toward me. "Money's
yours, fair and square!"

"What . . . but I didn't win . . ."

"Lord amighty, you are the dumbest creature on
God's green earth . . . not to mention, you give up
too easy."

She took my hand and placed it on the deck.

"Lift the top card," she said.

I did, and it was the ace of spades, all right. How the
hell she knew that, I'll never know. Maybe she was
Lady Luck, after all.

"You'll git it next time," she said, "and if you don't,
least you tried. You got magic in ya, all right—or call it
luck. I'm gonna let you pick out one of my best horses,
too . . . you'll find a whole pile of dead folks' saddles in

the shed. You can have some more greenbacks iffen you want . . . 'cept for this one."

And then in one gnarled little hand, my hundred-dollar bill, tucked away in a vest pocket, appeared; I recognized it by the pin holes.

"This here one I ain't never partin' with. Special feller gived it to me."

Impulsively, I stood and leaned across the stump and picked her up as if she were a child and kissed her on her wrinkled mouth. Tasted better than her stew, anyway.

Then I put her back down, and she whapped me on the ear again.

"Iffen I wanted to be kissed by strange men, d'ye think I'd become a durn hermit? And you're plenty strange, all right!"

She cackled with laughter at that; it was a ripsnorter.

When I rode off she was still sitting there, by the tree stump, a rattlesnake—Henry?—in her lap; she was stroking him, and she didn't wave.

But I did.

14

Riverboat Belle

The five-toned, full-throated whistle of the *Lauren Belle* bid St. Louis farewell, and the steamboat's bell in the pilot house clanged, both sounds echoing down the Mississippi River valley by way of warning and salutation. For a few moments, the whistle and bell overwhelmed even the uniformed brass band blaring away on the lower rail, just under the brilliant colorful banner that proclaimed WELCOME TO THE FIRST ANNUAL ALL-RIVERS POKER CHAMPIONSHIP.

The 250-foot steamboat's passenger list of three hundred was full—and yet the only destination was to go up-river, turn around, and come back again. With the exception of the handful of professional gamblers and foolish wealthy would-be poker experts—the contestants in this high-rolling affair—the passengers were spectators. You could bump into anyone from an English lord to an Episcopalian bishop, from a prosperous farmer to an equally prosperous politician. And you were apt to hear languages spoken from just about every country in Europe.

It was a well-dressed crowd, though few could compare to a certain handsome devil in string tie, red and black vest, black clawhammer coat, tan trousers, high-heeled fine leather boots, and (of course) a ruffled, white silk shirt straight from Paris, France, nice and roomy.

I'm sure I don't have to tell you his name.

I leaned against the railing, enjoying a cheroot and the way the sunlight dappled off the Mississippi. I'd seen a familiar face or two in the crowd, and one of them required special handling. I was contemplating that when I heard the familiar, lilting, and oh-so Southern tones of a certain young lady.

"Can it be?"

I turned, leaning my back to the rail, smiling. "It can, and it is. Hello, Annabelle."

She wore the same money-colored traveling costume, and for all she—and we—had been through, it looked none the worse for wear. Neither did she. She was lovely.

And she flew into my arms. "Oh, Bret . . . I've dreamed of this moment, prayed for this moment . . . my very own western hero . . . alive!"

"And well," I said, "no thanks to you."

I untangled myself from her.

"Have I said something to upset you?"

I turned away from her and looked back out at the river. St. Louis had receded and the greenery along either bank was soothing to the eye.

"Mrs. Bransford, I like to think I enjoy a good joke as well as the next fella, but stealing my savings before I rode off to face certain death among the savages? That's where my sense of humor ends."

She was beside me at the railing; she flicked the edge of my nearby frilly cuff. "You seem to have emerged unscathed. You even have two hands left, for playin' poker."

"For all the good they'd do me, without a stake."

Delicate fingers spread against her bosom. "Are you sayin' someone robbed you? How appallin'. Certainly you can't . . . you *don't* suspect . . . I can't bring myself to say it."

I'd almost forgotten how she could flutter those long lashes; almost.

"I don't suspect you," I said.

"I *am* relieved."

"I'm certain of it."

Now she was hurt.

"Bret," she said quaveringly, her Southern accent in full sway, "if you ever believed anything I ever told you, believe this . . . it was not I who took your money."

"I never did."

Hope sprang in the wide blue eyes. "You never thought I took your money?"

"I never did believe anything you ever told me."

She blinked, once. "Oh. Well, I *didn't* take it . . .

not then. Not when you were about to ride off so nobly with those hostiles."

"You did it earlier."

Her wide eyes held on me, and then went hooded, and she shrugged, and nodded. "I thought you were plannin' to take off without me, leavin' me behind with Coop and the prisoners and those settlers."

"Well, I was. But how does that justify you takin' my money?"

Her wince of guilt was almost convincing. "It doesn't, and I just feel ghastly about it."

"Not so 'ghastly' that you're offerin' to return my money, I notice."

"It's not mine to return. I only wish I could . . . it's wasted, now."

I frowned. "Why wasted?"

"The Commodore, that charming rattlesnake—"

"Please don't mention rattlesnakes. Go on. The Commodore?"

She smirked humorlessly. "I gave him my twenty-two thousand . . ."

"*Your* twenty-two thousand?"

"*Our* twenty-two thousand . . . we're partners, remember? I gave it to him, even though I was still shy three thousand, on the assumption I could raise the rest."

"Well, you haven't. Ask for it back."

"He agreed to reserve me a chair in the tournament, *and* allow a female to participate, only on the condition that should I fail to raise the full amount, my partial fee was non-returnable."

"That slick bastard. I suppose he made you put it in writing?"

She sighed and nodded. "I had hoped to find a wealthy inebriate or two I could flim-flam or pickpocket the meager remainder from, but alas, no luck. And I've only broken even these last few days, at the tables . . . despite your advice on my 'tells.' "

"At least you didn't lose . . . with the exception of 'our' twenty-two thousand, that is."

She shook her head and watched the shimmering water as the paddlewheeler propelled us up the Mississippi. "I don't mean to sound ungrateful, not to the most overwhelmin'ly attractive—"

"Please, Annabelle. Not after lunch."

"Sorry. Anyway, why'd you have to be three thousand short, Bret? My poor pure heart was so set on playing in this competition . . ."

I reached in my inside pocket, and pulled out the remaining sheaf of money my tiny benefactor had provided me.

Annabelle's eyes widened so much I thought Joseph and his braves were rowing toward us.

"Lady Luck has been kind to you, Bret."

Yes, she had.

"This is my twenty-five exactly," I said. I counted out three thousand in hundreds. "Here's the three you need."

She grabbed it out of my hands so fast for a moment I didn't think the money had ever been there.

"Is there no end to your sacrifice?" she asked.

"I'm a sucker for a pretty face with a sad story. Besides, it's the only way I can salvage part of 'our' twenty-two thousand. We're partners, Annabelle, and this time I agree with you."

"Agree?"

"Fifty-fifty's a fair split."

She didn't even argue as she put the bills in her purse. "Heaven will welcome you for this."

"Not too soon, I hope."

"Speaking of which . . . how ever did you escape those fearsome savages?"

"Got 'em drunk on firewater and slipped out in the confusion."

She beamed at the thought. "How could I not adore you?"

Joseph was right: white people will believe anything.

"But now you won't be able to enter the championship!" she said, and I almost believed she cared.

"Don't bet on it," I said, giving her a peck of a kiss on the forehead.

I found him on the upper deck, enjoying the view of this strange American wilderness he was visiting. He wore a three-piece herringbone suit with spats, white gloves, and top hat.

When I latched onto his shoulder, hard, and spun him around, his monocle dropped off even as his mouth dropped open, and his watch fob flapped and jingled.

The archduke, indignant and possibly a little afraid, said, "What is the meaning of this affront? Have you the least notion who—"

"I know exactly who you are, archduke," I said. "I've been tracking you for days. The question is—do you know who *I* am?"

He tried to keep the indignation going, but fear was winning out; as he studied me with glazed eyes, it was clear he didn't recognize the late Running Vulture, come back to life.

So I introduced myself.

"Bret Maverick," I said. "United States Government agent, Indian Affairs Bureau."

"Indian . . ."

I took him by the arm and began dragging him along. The other passengers were watching with interest but not alarm. "It's the end of the trail, Dukey . . . Joseph spilled the beans."

"What beans? Who on earth is 'Joseph'? I know no person by that name!"

I stopped, but still gripped his arm; looking him in the eye, I said, "Joseph is the Christian name taken by Screaming Eagle of Fakawi tribe."

The archduke began to reply, but no words came from his open trap-door of a mouth.

"Joseph denied knowing you, as well," I said, "when I first started investigating the murder of that poor savage. But putting the chief behind bars loosened his tongue. Maybe the same will be true with you."

I pulled him along, amid the stares and whispers of other passengers.

"But I am not an American," the archduke said.

"And lucky for you, too. Killing an Indian for sport, why that's a twenty-year sentence." I shook my head. "For a foreigner like you, with a certain diplomatic status, it's just a measly three years."

"Three years."

"Unless you decide to pay the three-thousand-dollar

fine, of course." I shrugged. "But that's between you and the judge."

"The judge?"

"Circuit judge. We're headin' back to Indian territory, you and me, and we'll put you in the pokey, for safekeepin', and then in six months or so, the judge'll come riding through. You can pay your fine then."

He stopped, and I allowed myself to stop, too, looking at him irritably.

"But Mr. Maverick," the archduke said, his eyes almost teary. He was desperate. "I *have* three thousand dollars. I have it right here."

He dug his wallet out from inside his fancy jacket.

I looked down my nose at him and his money. "Archduke—I'm disappointed in you. Do you know the penalty for bribing an agent of the United States Government?"

He shook his head vigorously. "It's *not* a bribe. It's my *fine*. I'm due to go home, soon—sooner! If you could pay my fine for me, it would save you and your government the cost of a trial."

I still wasn't sure. "How do you know I wouldn't just pocket this money?"

He gestured with open hands. "But you're an agent of the United States government—*of course* I can trust you."

I gave him a tentative smile. "Well, you're right about that. After all, if you can't trust an agent of the United States government, who can you trust?"

I took the money, and gestured for him to go.

"On second thought," he said, hesitating, "you do look familiar, somehow . . ."

"Naturally I look familiar," I snapped. "I'm your conscience!"

Not wanting to spend any more time with his conscience than necessary, he scurried away, and that was the last I ever saw of him.

Later I did hear talk, however, of a distinguished-looking gentleman in a monocle being aided by a deckhand as he climbed in a small boat. Rowing back to St. Louis would be a snap for a sportsman like the archduke.

I went upstairs to find the Commodore and see about paying my entry fee. Along the way I encountered my favorite Southern belle.

I was counting my money. "Guess what? I'm entering, too."

She was impressed. "How did you manage findin' another three thousand so quickly?"

"Maybe I miscounted."

"I hardly think so." She put her hands together and batted those lashes at me. "In any case, I couldn't be more thrilled! It's such a joy being partners with such a resourceful man."

"Annabelle—I'm in for fifty percent of what *you* win. You're not in for *any* part of what I win."

She pouted. "Why, that hardly seems fair. But what's a helpless little gal like me to do about such an injustice?"

I shuddered to think.

15

Old Home Week

The main cabin of the *Lauren Belle* was a hundred-foot-long, high-ceilinged salon hung with glittering crystal chandeliers, ornate wooden scrollwork friezes, lavishly frescoed walls, and lush floral carpeting. A soothing, elegant setting that was hopping with more activity—and people—than your average rodeo.

On both sides of the room, bartenders behind endless mahogany bars were working frantically to supply the demands of the well-dressed, mostly male crowd, who were throwing down brandy smashes, mint juleps, French brandy, and of course, bourbon, gin, and rum. A little band was going—fiddler, cornet player, fifer, and pianist at an upright; they were playing "Sweet Betsy from Pike," at the moment, not terribly well, mostly just working to be heard above the clamor.

Toward the center of the room, a quiet at the heart of this storm, were four empty poker tables, leather armchairs awaiting the contestants. In their midst sat a big fat safe, perched there like a cast-iron chaperon. The other gaming tables, wheels-of-fortune, chuck-a-luck cages, and roulette wheels, normally in this casino room, had been moved out for the occasion.

I watched from a corner, where I had positioned myself as far away from the mob as possible. The din was unavoidable. Despite all the talk of magic, witchcraft, and luck, I felt edgy, uneasy. No one could know that, looking at me, of course. My poker face is second to none.

Annabelle spotted me and headed over, winding through the milling throng as smoothly as a gentle stream running through a rocky landscape. She wore a lovely blue gown with a matching beaded glass necklace at her throat, golden curls piled atop her head, ribboned back; the swell of her bodice attracted many a masculine eye.

Including mine, though I hoped my poker face extended to this situation, as well.

She didn't say hello—she just started right in.

"Now, I've memorized both 'tells' you told me about, banished 'em from my bein' . . . no more touchin' my fingers together, or flickin' my pearly whites with my pretty little fingernail. But if I'm goin' to come out on top o' this little frolic, I need to know if I have any other 'dead giveaways' "

"Why should I help you?"

Her eyes saucered. "Because we're partners! You have an investment in me, Bret—"

"We're adversaries, Annabelle. Plain and simple."

She was astounded. "Then why did you give me that three-thousand dollars?"

"Hedging my bet. Or maybe I just wanted you in the game, so I could have the personal pleasure of publicly ruining you."

"How very unkind," she said, stung. "Besides . . . a girl can get lucky."

"Anyway, about now, you should be worrying more about other people's 'tells' than your own."

She made a face. "You know more of these people than I do. This is heady compan'y for a little Atlanta girl."

I had to smile. "So it's back to Atlanta, now is it? Just take some time getting the feel of their play, that's all. And like my pappy used to say, 'If it's a big hand, underplay it; if it's second-rate, overplay it—that's poker.' "

"You make it sound so childishly simple."

"Bein' childish can be helpful, now and then. Bein' simple, never. Here's another thing Pappy told me, 'Never trust a card player in loose clothes.' If a thin feller has a paunch under his vest, or if somebody's just plain wearin' a vest but keeps it unbuttoned, or if a man has overly wide sleeves hangin' out his coat, that sort of thing—"

"Could be a holdout device?"

"Exactly. And if somebody asks for a rule clarification

before bettin', run and hide. He knows the rules all too well, and's planning to sucker you."

"Well, I know the rules of poker—"

"Once upon a time, on a riverboat not unlike this one, in a game of five-card stud, a charming young lady named Samantha Crawford, with a Southern accent every bit as charming as yours—and just as phony—beat my straight with a mangy pair."

"However did she manage that?"

"By pointin' out an obscure but very real rule of Hoyle that straights don't count in five-card stud unless it's been agreed to at the start of the game."

"Ah." She smiled. "I'll have to remember that."

"Don't try it on the Mississippi. That story's better known up and down this river than 'Little Red Riding Hood'."

A handsome, tall, trim gambler stepped out of the crowd; he had dapper duds even I might envy, and the second sunniest smile in the room.

"Thought you'd be here!" I said to him, and extended my hand. We shook warmly. "Mrs. Bransford, meet Mr. Smith."

"A pleasure," she said, extending her hand for a kiss, which he granted, and which she obviously relished.

He gazed into her eyes and said, "Peter Piper picked a peck of pickled peppers."

"How perfectly charmin'," a confused Annabelle said, fluttering her lashes, "and also bewilderin'."

"That's great," I told him. "You've really improved."

"Yeah, b-b-b-but how often d-d-d-d-does it cuh-cuh-cuh-come up in a guh-guh-guh-game?"

I shrugged. "Just keep workin' on it, Stutterin'."

He nodded, smiled at us both, and returned to the crowd.

Suddenly Annabelle clutched my arm and whispered, "Bret . . . isn't that the terrible man from the poker game at Crystal River?"

I hadn't noticed him before, despite his size, but he was wearing a dark suit and a bowler and looked respectable and, amazingly, clean. Even his scruffy black beard was trimmed.

But it was the Angel, all right.

I tapped him on the shoulder. "Excuse me. I'm afraid there are no animals allowed outside the freight hold."

He whirled, wearing the expected sneer, but it faded into incredulity and even, and how I savored this, a trace of fear.

"How the hell did you—"

"Maybe I'm a ghost."

The fear vanished; the eyes narrowed. "You're damn lucky we had to check our guns at the door."

"Maybe *you're* lucky. Maybe then I would've just shot you on sight."

He snorted a laugh. "You ain't got the nerve, Maverick."

"You'd be surprised the nerve a man develops when he survives a hangin'. Why were you tryin' to stop me from gettin' to this game, Angel? *Who* was tryin' to stop me?"

Behind him, winding through the crowd, were his cronies—the sidewider with the wandering eye and the rope—burned buzzard. They, too, wore fancier duds and had bathed; but it didn't make them human.

Angel had worked up a smile so menacing I almost wished I hadn't confronted him.

But all he said, before joining his boys and moving off toward the bar, was, "Maybe I just wanted to weed out the competition. Be a real pleasure playin' cards with you again, amigo."

I watched him go.

Annabelle said, "*He's* entering the competition? Where did *he* get twenty-five thousand?"

"Hard as it may be for you to believe, Annabelle, he may have stolen it. I don't mean to bruise your delicate sensibilities, but there are dishonest people in this world."

On the other hand, maybe he got the money from whoever paid him to stop me from coming here.

"It's starting to feel like old home week," I said.

But Annabelle wasn't at my side; she was off to my left, speaking to someone.

"He got them all drunk on firewater and slipped away in the confusion," she was saying.

"Never lost faith in the boy," Coop said. "He's a good man, underneath that womanly shirt."

I'd never seen him look braver or tougher or more formidable. To his fancy-dan apparel had been added several telling touches: a wide-brimmed white Stetson and a glittering marshal's badge. Also, his holstered sidearm had been replaced by twin holstered Colts with pearl handles, both tied down in the shootist manner.

"*Two* guns?" I said, coming over.

He smiled, just a little. "When I'm travelin', I go light. But when I'm workin', I heavy it up a mite."

"Working?" I said.

"Working," he said. "What took you so long to get here, son?"

"It's a long story," I said, but the story would have to wait, because a gong sounded, startling the room, quieting it down but for a burst or two of nervous laughter. A powerful-looking ship's steward was responsible, up toward the front of the room, and he struck it again, silencing even the sweat-soaked musicians, who'd been caught midstream in "The Yellow Rose of Texas."

Coming up out of the crowd and onto a small platform shared by the steward and his gong was a tall, slender, energetic man of perhaps fifty, impeccably dressed in a gray three-piece suit, the gleaming diamond stickpin in his cravat visible even from the back of the room, where we were standing.

Just as visible, and as gleaming, was his irresistible smile in a well-groomed gray beard, a smile as wide as the river, and twice as treacherous. His eyes had the same gleam, and the crowd loved him, though they knew he was an unrepentant rascal.

He was Commodore George Devol, a much-storied gambler who was said to have earned at least two million in his career, up and down this river. Much of it he'd lost, but some of it he had sunk into the floating casino that was the *Lauren Belle*.

"Welcome," he said, gesturing with a hand that held a slender cheroot between fingers glistening with diamond rings, "to the *Lauren Belle*, and our first-ever annual poker championship. Some of you may be wondering why I would go to the trouble of mountin' such a competition, and the answer is quite simple . . . at risk of being considered a poor host, I must admit I have every intention of winning the damn thing myself!"

He smiled and there was murmured laughter among the crowd; but every man (and woman, too) knew the Commodore was capable of just that. Though three-card monte had built his fortune, the Commodore was a poker man, through and through.

"Most of you know me," he said easily. "Some of you even like me. Some of you are fools, just bein' here—and how much crossover there is among those last two groups, I leave for others, less biased than myself, to decide."

Hearty, good-hearted laughter rumbled around the room; but I wasn't smiling.

"The truth is this," the Commodore was saying, pacing like a panther up on that platform, "I'm both a great businessman *and* a great poker player. This, along with my equally great natural modesty, has brought all of you fine folks onto my ship."

The crowd was getting restless. The Commodore had crowded enough; time to get down to business.

He sensed that, and did. "The rules are elegant in their simplicity: we play till we drop. We alternate rounds of draw, five- and seven-card stud. Winner takes all. House deals, and only a dealer can call for a break."

"How long a break?" someone called out.

"Half an hour, and there's only gonna be one of 'em. If a player ain't back in time, he's out. Soon as you're busted, you're gone . . . no buyin' back in. Twenty of us are playin', which means by mornin', there's gonna be countless dashed hopes and nineteen broken hearts

. . . 'specially when *I* win the half million in cash that's at stake."

The crowd began to murmur and mutter again; half a million dollars was a fortune that made any other high-stakes poker game in the history of the West—or anyplace else, for that matter—recede into insignificance.

A well-dressed little man nearby noticed me and tipped his derby; I nodded back.

"Never try to read *him*," I whispered to Annabelle.

"Oh?"

"His nickname is 'Twitchy.' "

"Oh."

Up front, the Commodore was calling for quiet.

When he got it, he continued. "To those of you participating, I want to point out that every spectator here has paid a hundred dollars for the privilege. So be polite to 'em, and let's make it a great contest, and a hell of a show!"

Applause started up, but the Commodore patted the air and stopped it.

"Not just a great contest, but an *honest* one, and for that reason, I have brought in a legend of the West, one of our most celebrated lawmen . . . *Marshal Zane Cooper!* Come on up here, Coop."

Now the applause was deafening as Coop, nearby, smiled in his aw-shucks manner and moved through a crowd that got out of his way, eyes full of awe, like he was all the Earp boys rolled into one with a little Wild Bill Hickock tossed in for good measure.

Coop moved up on the little stage next to his beaming, bearded host, and gave the crowd a winning smile.

"Thank you, Commodore. Thank you kindly, gentlemen, and ladies . . . there *are* a few ladies present, I see."

Mild laughter stopped cold when Coop's expression turned suddenly grave.

"Anyone caught cheating forfeits their entrance fee and is banned from the game," he said. "And I will personally throw them overboard."

The silence was like a heavy cloud hanging over the salon.

Coop unbuttoned his jacket and let them see the twin Colts holstered at his sides, tied to his thighs. "See these? These are the only guns allowed in this room. Any others, any fancy little derringers you might have tucked away in a boot or a sleeve, I see 'em, their owners are out of the game. Spectators seen bearin' arms are off the ship. I'm the law in this room, friends, and anyone breaking the law, as I see it, risks me breaking their bones."

Then he smiled again, tipped his Stetson, said, "Thank you kindly," and stepped down into the hushed, wary crowd.

"Thank you, Marshal," the Commodore said. "Now—contestants, please step forward . . . and bring your money!"

Soon Annabelle and I were in line near one of the poker tables where the Commodore and Coop sat, taking the entrance fees, counting the money, issuing receipts.

When we got up to the front of the line, the Commodore took my money and said, "Well, Bret Maverick.

Glad to have you in the game. No hard feelings, I hope."

"Why should there be hard feelings?"

"Well . . . I believe your brother Bart felt I did him an injustice in this very room, not no long ago."

"He lost a big pot to you. Happens all the time."

"Not to a Maverick. At any rate, glad to have you aboard. Ah! Miss Bransford . . ."

"Mrs. Bransford," she corrected gently.

"My mistake," the Commodore said. "Have you come up with the balance of your entry fee?"

"I have," she said, and gave him the pile of hundred-dollar bills.

"How pleased I am," the Commodore said, handing the money to Coop to count.

I leaned in, so only the Commodore could hear. "I staked her to this game."

An eyebrow arched; his smile in the well-trimmed beard was guarded. "Really?"

"I wanted to lay my cards straight up. If you have a problem with one player bankrollin' another, say so now."

Annabelle, catching pieces of this, pressed in. "What are you *sayin'*, Bret?"

"If you don't want her in the game," I said, " 'cause she's playin' on my money, well . . . now's the time to say so."

His eyes narrowed, skeptically. "But Miss—Mrs. Bransford understood that she would forfeit—"

"No," I said. "She was to forfeit only if she didn't raise the balance of the entry fee. She did that very thing—you hold the money in your hand, Commodore."

He thought about it. "So it is. So it is." He turned to Coop. "What do you think, Marshal?"

"That boy is something I never thought I'd see," Coop said quietly. "An honest gambler."

I grinned. "My pappy wouldn't like hearing me referred to as a gambler, but thanks for the vote of confidence, anyway."

Coop nodded, his faint smile like a benediction.

"All right," the Commodore said, "you're both in the game. But I'll instruct my dealers to watch to see if either of you favors or aids the other in any way."

"Don't worry, Commodore," I said, grinning again, "that's one thing Mrs. Bransford and I *never* do."

When all the entrants had paid their fee, Coop counted the money one last time—pronouncing it half a million dollars. He produced a satchel he'd brought himself, to which he held the only key, and the room watched as all that money was deposited in the safe.

Coop shut the safe's door with a decisive *thud*, twirled the dial, and said, "The lock on this safe was constructed especially for this competition, and only I know its combination. No one else aboard, not even the Commodore himself, knows it."

"Thank you, Marshal," the Commodore said, "for these stalwart efforts."

"If there's any other way to protect this money," Coop admitted frankly, "I'll be hornswoggled if I know what it is."

The contestants, and spectators too, were gathered around the safe, gazing at it in a unique conmingling of near-religious fervor and abject lust.

"Gentlemen," the Commodore said. "Mrs. Bransford . . . if you will go to your assigned tables, we will begin."

16

Wheel of Fortune

After a word of prayer from Coop and a collective, "Amen," we fanned out, taking our assigned seats, as the white-shirted, garter-sleeved, professional dealers at each table solemnly opened new decks and began shuffling cards.

My pocket watch said six o'clock, and the bongs of a grandfather's clock agreed with it. The crowd of spectators, already well-oiled, gathered 'round us, liquor glasses in hand. Stutterin' Smith sat next to me, with three other players, as well as a pockmarked dealer who looked older and rougher than those at the other tables. That was all right with me: he also wore a mantle of experience.

Annabelle was seated at the table nearest me, my wealthy little friend Twitchy sitting right across from her, gazing at her dreamily, spellbound by her beauty. Lovesick or not, it wouldn't take Twitchy long to live up to his nickname and present that very special symphony of tics, shrugs, grimaces, blinks, mutterings, and fidgeting that made him so impossible to read.

At another table were two familiar faces—Commodore Devol and the Angel. Actually, I knew damn near all the professional players here. An exception was the sweet-faced fancy pants sitting opposite me who, judging by his table chatter, was from out in mining country, where I was less-traveled.

It was the rich men, who fancied themselves players, that were strangers to me—like the white-bearded old coot in the baggy plaid shirt, who alluded to the fortune in gold he'd dug out of the earth. All this meant, really, was that I'd have to use my normal strategy of playing awhile to get the feel of the game.

Problem with that strategy was, as the evening would progress, and players went bust and dropped out, the number of tables would thin, and players from one table would join another, the cast of characters constantly shifting, the complexion of the game always changing.

In addition, there were some damn fine players here—nerves of steel, and keen-as-a-Bowie-knife poker minds—the Commodore himself, for one. I could hear my pappy's voice saying, "Son, if you ever find yourself

in a game with men who play as smart as you, quit—
that's gamblin'."

But the game was just starting, and I was in for the
duration—or at least till Lady Luck booted me out.

The worst part of it, at first, were the damn spectators, eavesdropping, peeking over our shoulders, whispering to each other, occasionally making comments
they shouldn't. I shot Coop a glance, early on, and he
made a point of telling the audience to keep their
observations to themselves.

"Check," I said.

Next to me Stutterin' was trying to form a word; he
glanced at me for help.

"Stutterin' checks," I said.

From time to time, when I'd folded early, I'd watch
Annabelle. She had her tells reined in pretty good,
seemed to be playing very professionally, pulling in a lot
of pots, some of them pretty good-sized.

It was around to Stutterin' again.

He gave me an urgent look, and tightened his eyes,
then untightened them, and tightened them again.
An almost imperceptible gesture, but I'd played with
Stutterin' a lot of times, and we were friends.

"Stutterin' raises two hundred," I said.

When he pulled in his nice big pot, Stutterin' cackled
like a fool; didn't seem to require any help doing that.

Beyond the windows of the salon, twilight was settling gently on the river, as the sternwheeler churned
upstream. A swirling haze of cigar, cigarette, and pipe
smoke, hanging over the room, might have been fog.
The grandfather clock bonged seven times.

That sweet-faced fancy pants right across from me,

his expression was just too innocent for an honest man; and that lovely shirt of his, poking out stiff from his coat sleeves, had much wider cuffs than current fashion decried.

I'd watched him long enough to be sure about it. I folded my hand, stretched, yawned, and strolled over to Coop, who, thumbs in his gun belt, was prowling the playing area like it was the main street of Dodge.

I whispered to him, and he nodded, and I went back to my chair in plenty of time for the next hand. The crowd was getting drunk and sleepy; a few rowdy sorts had already had their behinds tossed out of there by Coop. The little band of musicians seemed never to stop, though I had heard far more spirited renditions of "Little Brown Jug" than the one they'd been working at for the past ten or fifteen minutes.

The sweet-faced fancy pants was half out of his chair, reaching out to sweep in the chips of an enormous pot with those wide-cuffed hands of his. He had settled back in his chair when Coop dropped a powerful hand on his shoulder, and leaned in to whisper a word or two in his ear.

"Me?" the gambler said, a picture of shocked innocence.

Coop just looked at him; then he curled his forefinger as if summoning a naughty child.

The man's face wasn't so sweet as he sighed indignantly and stood, only to have Coop haul him by the arm over to a corner of the room. A few eyes were too preoccupied with their cards to look, but every other orb was fixed on the sight of Coop practically ripping Fancy Pants's jacket off, and literally ripping off the left wide-cuffed sleeve of his shirt, revealing the metal-and-leather holdout device buckled around his bare arm.

Wearing one of those, all you had to do was bend your elbow, and a hidden-away card would slip into your palm, the device retracting via a system of rubber bands.

Then Coop was hauling him out of the salon, and a few moments later there were two sounds: a howl, and a splash. A big one.

When Coop came back in, he returned to our table, waited until we'd finished our latest hand, then gestured to the empty chair.

"Sudden case of sea sickness, gents." He pushed our departed compatriot's chips into the center of the table. "Divide those up equal amongst yourselves. House rules."

Coop glanced at me, our gazes locked for a moment or two, and we exchanged nods of thanks.

Then it was back to the game.

By the time the grandfather clock bonged ten, the river out the window was shining in the moonlight, the spectators were fading and thinning out, and the little band of musicians were playing everything at a dirge tempo. We were down to four tables. Fifteen players.

I could see Annabelle was tiring. She'd never been in a marathon game before, and I felt bad for not warning her. Seeing her trying to relax, breathing deeply, rubbing her eyes, I knew she was in for a hard time. She was winning, piles of chips before her, but her stamina was waning.

By two in the morning, the spectators were all but

gone, just a few drunk hangers-on remaining. We were down to two tables—both Stutterin' and Twitchy were among the five players at mine; Annabelle was sharing a table with Commodore Devol and the Angel, and two others.

I was playing smart, conservative poker; I'd won a number of big pots—a jacks over queens full house had proved as profitable as it was pretty—and I was just about where I wanted to be, at this stage of the game.

The only problem was, I was tired.

A few hours ago, I'd been worrying about Annabelle, but she seemed to have gotten a second wind. Me, my back was aching, my shoulders felt tight, even my arms were tired; my skin was sticky from sweat, my eyes burning due to the tobacco smoke. Sometimes I could barely focus enough to just see my cards, let alone concentrate on their meaning, their value, their consequences. . . .

The old coot in the plaid shirt was apparently having the same problem. He'd stopped blathering about his gold mine a few hands ago, and shifted subjects to how exhausted he was. At times, he would practically double over like a man about to fall asleep, or stretch and extend his legs, trying to keep his circulation going.

But his eyes were bright.

A little too bright, and I gave Coop a nod.

"I cain't hardly remember my own name no more," the coot was saying, then pointed at an already generous pot. "What is it to me?"

Our pockmarked hardbitten dealer—who, next to Coop possibly, seemed in better shape than any of us—said, "Three thousand to you."

"Can I raise ten thousand?"

The dealer didn't give a damn. "Up to you, gramps."

"Well, then," the coot said cheerily, "why don't I jest do that . . ."

And he pushed a pile of chips out to the center of the table.

Everybody else folded, with groans of disgust, with one exception: Coop was still in the game. So to speak. He grabbed the old guy by the arm and yanked him away from the table. We watched with keen interest, considering the shape we were all in, as Coop ripped the codger's plaid shirt open and revealed a breastplate holdout sewn inside.

You could produce, or conceal, an entire hand of cards with one of those gadgets; all you had to do was bend or stretch your leg to work the long cord that went down into your boot.

Another howl, another splash, some cheater's chips passed around to replenish us, and we were back in the game.

My pocket watch said it would be four in the morning soon, and I wasn't the only one having trouble staying alert; people were openly rubbing their arms, their eyes, stretching limbs, and it didn't have anything to do with cheating—just trying to stay awake, if not sharp.

Annabelle's second wind was serving her well: she was winning, and winning handily. But the Commodore, and even the Angel, were big winners, too. The only person with more chips than those three, at either of the tables, was me.

Even our tough-as-nails dealer was starting to fade.

The grandfather clock bonged four, and that was all he needed to hear.

"Break," he said, standing, tossing the deck of cards on the table. "Anyone not back in half an hour, sharp, is out of the game."

You could have fueled the steamboat for five miles with the collected sighs of relief.

I would imagine anybody walking past my state-room—hearing me groaning with pleasure, not to mention the continual squeal of bedsprings—might have got the wrong idea.

"You are so good," I told Annabelle. "Don't stop . . I'll just die if you stop . . . ."

"What am I worth?"

"Five hundred. No—a thousand!"

I was face-down on my mattress and Annabelle, her gown hiked up, was straddling my waist, using her delicate and gifted fingers to massage the aching muscles of my back, shoulders, and neck.

Then she stopped, hopped off, and swatted me on the behind.

"My turn," she said.

My face was still in the pillow; my voice muffled, but audible: "Two thousand in chips, if you keep it up."

"No good," she said. "I got chips. Right now I need my back rubbed more."

I hauled myself off the mattress, allowed her to flop down in my place, and I sat on the edge of the bed and massaged her back, which was surprisingly muscular.

"Hell," I grumbled, "you're in better shape than I am."

"Know how I got that way? Doin' the laundry of such an overwhelmin'ly attractive—ouch!"

"Sorry."

An insistent pounding rattled the wooden door of the little stateroom.

"It's open," I said.

Coop stepped in, Stetson in hand. At the sight of me rubbing Annabelle's back, he raised an eyebrow, but just for a moment. He seemed preoccupied.

"I was gettin' a little tired," he said, "so I decided to stretch my legs."

"You?" I said. "A legend of the West, tired? That's a first."

"Listen up." His expression, his voice, were tight with urgency and concern. "I was leaning against the rail, takin' some air, and overheard these two varmints talkin' . . . and they *are* varmints."

I was on my feet now. "Who do you mean?"

"That scruffy scoundrel they call the Angel, and the dealer at your table . . . the hardcase? They were putting their heads together, scheming about something, and your name come up."

"What did you hear, exactly?"

Coop shook his head, disgustedly. "No details. But I did hear one thing clear: the Angel tellin' that dealer he had to make *damn* sure you don't win."

Annabelle was next to me now, touching my arm. "Are you all right, Bret?"

I nodded. "Thanks, Coop."

He nodded. "What do you intend to do about it?"

Their eyes were on me.

"Take a quick nap," I said. "If someone's going to try to cheat me, well, I better at least be rested."

Annabelle took Coop's arm. "Escort me to my room, would you, Marshal Cooper? I'd like to freshen up a little myself. Bret? Would you like me to knock on your door as I pass, and make sure you don't sleep through the game?"

"I'd appreciate it."

Her smile was lovely and she batted those lashes. "Not that it really matters, or these fellas plannin' to cheat you, either. After all, *I'm* the one who's goin' to win this match, so why make worry lines on your handsome brow?"

And they were gone.

I didn't sleep, just rested, cleared my head, and listened to the churning of water from the paddlewheel just outside the porthole. Now and then I checked my pocket watch.

At four-twenty, someone knocked, sharply, at my stateroom door.

"Bret?" came Annabelle's voice. "The Marshal and I are headin' back to the main salon. Care to join us?"

"No thanks," I said, sitting on the edge of the bed. "See you in a couple minutes."

"Suit yourself," she said.

I splashed some water on my face from the basin on a compact bureau (there was barely room to turn around in the little cabin) and then I thought I heard someone else at my door. Not a knock, but something that seemed to bump up against it.

I went to the door. "Yes?"

No reply.

I tried to open it, but it wouldn't budge. Had I locked it? No. Why wouldn't it budge?

"Annabelle, open the damn door!"

I pulled at the handle, put all my strength into it, to no avail. If it wasn't locked, then somebody had wedged something under the handle—a chair maybe? That wouldn't be Annabelle's doing; not her style. Maybe this was what Angel and that dealer had cooked up for me.

At any rate, checking my pocket watch and seeing that I had just a little less than four minutes to get back to the game or be tossed the hell out of it, I had to improvise.

I went to the porthole, beyond which the enormous wooden paddlewheel made its circuit; just above me was the main salon, not far away at all. I popped open the little round window and water splashed in gently, and it seemed almost refreshing; could have saved myself the trouble of splashing myself from that basin.

I stuck my head out. Was there room between the paddlewheel and the side of the ship for me to climb up there, and was there anything to hold on to?

Between here and the railing of the upper deck balcony was a flagpole bearing a *Lauren Belle* banner, a blue banner turned copper-colored in the smoky glow of the brass kerosene-burning firepots. The pole loomed far enough above the paddlewheel to avoid its splatter, well out of my reach. Also, there were some guy wires.

I could think of only one way to get up there, and I hated it. I checked my pocket watch: 4:28. Two minutes and I was bust. As Pappy used to say, "Life's saddest truth is you can only play the hand you're dealt."

And I wasn't about to fold.

So I left my pocket watch behind on the bureau, and climbed up and through that porthole into the misty kiss of the paddlewheel as it revolved. It was snug, and hurt like hell, and for one long, dreadful moment I was stuck there.

But with my hands against the cool, water-slick side of the boat, I could push, and push I did, until I'd squeezed through, and sat with my ass hanging out the little window, the paddlewheel at my back, inches away.

Hanging onto a guy wire, I maneuvered into position, the heels of my boots hooked on the porthole as I reached up for the flagpole. I stretched, slipped, and damn near lost my balance, but thanks to the guy wire, I was saved from a tumble into those churning paddlewheel blades.

Then I jumped toward that flagpole and latched on like a monkey in the jungle on a branch, and I swung the same way, and swung again, and made a monkey of myself once more, sending myself skimming over those paddlewheel blades, water spraying me, skirting the firepots, and when I was near that upper deck railing, I let go.

I flew over the rail and landed in an unceremonious pile on the deck. Then I got to my feet and walked quickly to the main doors and into the salon, where an obviously worried Coop and Annabelle reacted with surprise and relief.

I was damn near soaking wet, and my heart was beating like a jackrabbit's, but I was on time.

As I sat my damp behind on the leather chair, the

granfather clock began to bong on the half hour, and I called a waiter over.

"Could you get me a towel, please?" Then I gave my sunniest smile to the others at my table—my friends Stutterin' and Twitchy, but most of all, the glowering hardbitten dealer.

"Nothing more invigorating than a moonlight swim, gentlemen. Shall we play poker?"

17

Hand of Luck

By half-past-five, dawn streaking through the windows like swords piercing a magician's box, six poker players sat at one table—the only table now. To the dealer's left was Stutterin' Smith, then Twitchy, Commodore Devol, the Angel, Annabelle, and me.

The men looked bleary-eyed and bone-weary; we needed shaves, we needed sleep, we needed better-tasting coffee than the mud the Commodore's waiters were setting down beside us.

Annabelle, however, had returned from the break looking refreshed, as if she'd been replaced by a twin sister who'd been resting up in her cabin during the initial hours of the competition. She had exchanged her gown for a traveling costume, under the jacket of which was a crisp, shirtwaist-style blouse. Her hair was combed and lovely, and she had reapplied her make-up with her usual tasteful restraint. It was hard not to fall in love with her, and easy to hate her.

Coop sat on the edge of one of the now-vacant tables, arms folded, eyes trained on us like a cavalry sentry watching the horizon for hostiles. A few spectators were drifting in, having caught an hour or two of sleep and somehow managing to wake themselves up, so as not to miss the finish of the big game. They looked like hell—hung-over, puffy-faced, wobbly-kneed; and somehow it was reassuring, seeing somebody who felt worse than you did.

Of the spectators, the ones who looked the freshest were Angel's two sidekicks, the wandering-eyed sidewinder and the rope-burned buzzard. They hadn't been drinking as much as most in the audience last night, and had disappeared around two, apparently to catch some shut-eye. It was as if Angel had instructed them to stay sober and alert, and be in for the finish.

Maybe he had.

I was out in front, chips piled tidily before me, but my lynch-party buddy Angel was coming up right behind me. The Commodore and Twitchy were holding their own, though Annabelle—for all her freshness— was having trouble. Stutterin's neatly stacked chips were dwindling, too.

Within a few hands, Annabelle's pile of chips had shrunk worse than that shirt of mine she'd laundered.

Next hand, it was down to just the two of us,

Annabelle and me, and the bet was to her. She was appraising her cards, cool, confident, collected, not revealing a damn thing.

Then, with an endearing little toss of her head, which made her blond curls bounce, she said to the uninterested dealer, "Can I bet everything I have left?"

He nodded, boredom his burden in life.

"Then why don't I do that little thing?" she pushed her chips out into the center of the table.

"How much is that?" I asked.

"Five thousand, Mr. Maverick," she said, and her expression was blank as a baby's.

I was proud of her. She had her "tells" under control. All except one I hadn't told her about, of course.

"Have to be a damn fool to buck that kind of confidence," I said.

She just looked at me. I'll be damned if I wasn't making a poker player out of her.

Anyway, for a second or two, I let her think I was seriously considering folding, just to be ornery, then said, "Well, I guess I just feel like bein' a damn fool, this mornin' . . . I'll call."

I counted out five thousand in chips and pushed them into the pot.

"All you have to do," I said, showing her my hand, "is beat tens and threes."

She scowled and threw her cards in. "Bastard!"

I shrugged and leaned over to pull in the pot.

"That puts me out of the game," she said, and stood.

The other men at the table stood, and nodded politely to her, mumbling, "Pleasure playin' with you," and the like. Me, I was busy counting and stacking the chips I'd just won off her.

She came around and whispered harshly in my ear. "You no-account bastard, you put me out of the game!"

"You were bluffing."

"I didn't do *either* of my tells, all night long! Never touched my thumbnail with my little finger, nor flicked my teeth . . ."

I was holding up a stack of red chips, counting them. "You have *three* dead giveaways."

"Three!"

"You always toss your head and raise your chin before you bluff. It's cute as hell."

"You didn't tell me that one!"

"Like Pappy used to say, 'Never show your hole card, less'n some fool pays to see it.' "

"Well," she huffed, "you can just go straight to hell, Mr. Bret Maverick!"

Then she stood and tossed her pretty curls and raised her chin, but I don't think she was bluffing. "I'll just have to pretend all that money I lost belonged to somebody else."

Taking a deep breath, she regained her dignity, her poise, her self-control, and smiled graciously.

"Thank you for a most enjoyable evenin', Commodore," she said, and joined Coop at the nearby, otherwise vacant table. Most of the eyes at the table were on her as she went, pretty thing that she was.

But I saw Angel and that hardbitten dealer exchange a glance; a telling glance, at that.

Coop may have caught it, too, but I was pretty sure

Angel and the dealer thought their casual little signal had gone unnoticed.

At any rate, Coop stood and began circling the table, checking, eyes on everybody, including the dealer, who seemed to be his usual bored, detached self, business as usual, casually shuffling the cards for yet another round of draw.

I wasn't sure whether Coop saw what I saw, and the dealer probably didn't know how close I was watching him, as I seemed to be preoccupied with stacking and re-stacking my chips.

But I was watching him, all right, and he was a brilliant mechanic. He'd been dealing straight all night—though I'd been watching him close from the first hand, because he had the woman-soft hands and sandpapered fingertips of the card sharp.

And, by God, he was good. It takes dexterity to make the cards do what you want them to, and nerve to do it in front the watchful eyes of professional gamblers. Sure, we were tired, and we were bleary-eyed, but we weren't easily cheated, our kind.

As he dealt out our cards, he took them sometimes from the top, sometimes the bottom, sometimes the second card, sometimes the third, and sometimes from the middle of the deck, which (as Pappy used to put it) is "harder than a blind man bustin' a bronco."

Did anyone else at the table notice? No one seemed to.

I had a good hand, for draw, particularly since we weren't playing jacks-or-better to open; all you needed to open was guts, and I had better than guts: I had the ten, jack, queen, king—all of spades.

Odds on improving an open-ended straight flush were two to one. Drawing a nine, or an ace, was a fairly long shot—twenty-two and a half to one; but a seductive long shot.

If this were an honest hand, in an honest game, I knew how I'd play it.

But since these cards had been carefully selected by the dealer just for me, that gave the game a different spin entirely.

Looking at my fellow players, I saw poker faces working so hard to be poker faces that I almost smiled; even Twitchy had his tics under control. *I knew what that slick bastard of a dealer had done.* But I bided my time, to get my suspicion confirmed.

Didn't take long.

"How many cards?" the bored dealer asked Stutterin'.

Stutterin' glanced at me and widened his eyes, almost imperceptibly.

"Stutterin' stands pat," I said.

"Cards?" the dealer said to Twitchy.

"Happy with these," Twitchy said.

The dealer turned to the Commodore, who smiled big and said, "I don't believe these could be improved upon."

Then it was to Angel, who asked for—and got—one card. Actually, he got the third card from the top, but who was counting?

Three pat hands, and Angel asks for one card. That could only mean one thing: the dealer had fed "unbeatable" pat hands to the first three, and had just filled an even more "unbeatable" hand with the card he'd given his cohort, Angel.

The card the dealer would find for me, in his friend the deck, would of course not fill my straight flush, but it would complete my flush, or my straight—just enough to keep me in for the kill.

"Maverick?" the dealer said impatiently.

"I want one card," I said, and his hand was moving to the deck, to find me just the right wrong card, when I placed my hand over his and stopped the deal.

"What—?"

"I said I want a card—but I don't want it from you."

The room stirred.

The Commodore said, "What are you tryin' to pull, son?"

The dealer wasn't saying anything; for all his toughness, for all the harshness of his pockmarked features, he had fear in his eyes. Because my eyes were boring right into his, and told him I knew exactly what he'd been up to.

No emotion in my voice whatsoever, I said, "I want a new dealer—and I want a new shuffle. And a new cut."

The Commodore said, "I don't know if this is—"

Coop interrupted; maybe he had spotted the fancy card-handling, after all. He said, coldly, firmly, "The boy is within his rights. *I'll* shuffle."

The Commodore sighed, nodded. "All right, then. I'll cut."

"No," I said. I looked at Angel and smiled the sunny smile. "Let *him* cut."

The Angel's smile was not at all sunny. "I kinda like that, Maverick. Shows trust."

Coop moved the dealer out of his chair, roughly, and sat and shuffled the cards, a bit clumsily. Then he slapped them in front of Angel.

Even a percentage player has to go with luck, sometimes. I closed my eyes, and listened: I thought I could hear the wind again, outside that strange little old gal's cabin, whispering encouragement, and I thought about magic, and witchcraft, and just plain luck.

Angel's huge hand settled on the deck, blotting it out, making two piles of cards out of it. I reached my hand over gently and made it a deck again.

The Angel, grinning his hideous yellow grin, pushed a thick finger against the top card, sliding it off the deck, and over in front of me. Face-down, of course.

I left it there, like that.

Coop said, "I believe the bet is yours, Mr. Smith."

Stutterin' held up two forefingers, and I said, "Stutterin' bets two thousand."

Twitchy didn't twitch; he just called. I could tell the little man wanted to raise, but he just didn't have enough chips in front of him to chance it. At this stage of the game, all it would take to get rid of him—and Stutterin', for that matter—would be for one of the rest of us to make a raise they couldn't match.

What they had contributed to the pot, to that point, would be just that: a contribution.

And that was the way we were heading, because the Commodore, flashing that irresistible smile, said, "And raise five thousand."

The pile of chips in the center of the table was impressive, and getting more impressive all the time.

By the way, I hadn't looked at that card yet, and

everybody knew it. It was still face-down on the table, and driving the rest of them crazy.

Angel pretended he was trying to decide whether his hand was worth staying in with or not; then he abandoned his strategy and leered yellowly at me.

"I liked what you done to that little lady," Angel said. "Poker's a man's game. Raise twenty thousand."

Gasps from the small, but intently watching, crowd drowned out various sighs from around the table. Stutterin' and Twitchy were entering dangerous territory.

I looked at the back of my fifth card; it looked back at me. Was it the ace of spades? The card of death? My ma's favorite card?

"I'd look at it 'fore you bet, son," the Commodore said.

I gave him half a smile. "My ole pappy said, 'Son—never trust advice given you over a poker table.' Of course, we were playin' cards at the time . . ."

"Are you in?" Coop asked.

"I'm workin' on it," I said, then I pushed piles of chips into the pot. "Call, and raise twenty-five."

Angel exploded. "You can't bet without lookin' at your goddamn card! What kind of trick are you tryin' to pull?"

I smiled amiably. "I don't believe there's anything in Hoyle that says I can't make a blind bet. And as for tricks, I know a good one . . . you put a chair up under the handle of somebody's stateroom door, and trap 'em inside."

Everybody at the table—everybody in the room—looked at me like I was a madman; but Angel just looked away, looked at his cards, and beads of sweat rolled from his greasy hair down his forehead and into the thicket of his black beard.

Stutterin' was counting his chips. He breathed a sigh of relief--he had just enough to stay in.

"Stutterin' calls," I said.

And he pushed his chips into the growing pile.

Twitchy gave Stutterin' an apologetic look, accompanied by a minor spasm. "Sorry," he said. "Raise two thousan'."

That meant the end of Stutterin', whose eyes spoke of the tragedy of holding a hand that was a sure thing, and not having the means to back it up to the finish line.

"I'm afraid we're saying goodbye to you, as well, Twitchy," the Commodore said, and he pushed every one of his chips in the pot. "Fifty thousand more."

The spectators, including Angel's boys, were on their feet, surrounding us; you could have heard a chip drop.

The Angel was smiling again. "You want to see me, Maverick, it'll cost you everything you got."

And his huge hands pushed towering piles of chips into the pot; if they'd been coins, not red, white and blue chips, I'd have thought I'd found the end of the rainbow.

"Hundred and fifty thousand," Angel said.

"Maybe next year," the Commodore said, and his dazzling smile was nowhere in sight. He sighed and threw in his cards. "Half a million in that pot, gentlemen, if Mr. Maverick decides to match it."

I hadn't looked at my last card yet.

Faint heart never filled a flush. Or a straight flush, either.

I pushed in all of my chips.

Eyes around the table were wide; heads were wagging in disbelief. Annabelle, watching me in the background, looked stunned.

Angel began to laugh; it was a booming laugh, with some growl in it, and no humor at all. With more melodrama than I figured him capable of, the big man turned over his cards, one at a time.

Five . . . six . . . seven . . . eight . . . nine.

All diamonds.

There were *oohs* and *ahs* from the stunned assemblage, and even a little applause. To those of us who love poker, a straight flush is a thing of beauty, though a relative beauty which does tend to shift according to which side of it you're sitting on.

Well, I had at least as good a sense of melodrama as the Angel, and so when I showed them my hand, it was one card at time, saving that face-down card that I hadn't touched yet, for last.

Even Angel seemed impressed by the sight of the ten of spades, jack of spades, queen of spades, and king of spades.

But without a nine, or an ace, they were pretty, but pretty harmless.

I didn't show them the last card yet; I wanted to look at it myself, first—after all, I was the one who paid for it. Wanted to make sure it was what I thought it was . . .

"Hell," I said, softly. And I shook my head. "Hell . . . I don't believe this . . ."

The Angel's obnoxious laughter rattled the fancy chandelier above as he leaned over and scooped the chips up in his big paws and started to drag them home.

"Don't cry, Maverick," he gloated. "Lotta hard-to-believe things happen at a poker table."

"I know. But whoever heard of two straight flushes in the same hand?"

I flipped the card in the air and it spun like the paddlewheel and landed face up.

"Lucky mine's higher," I said.

Ace of spades.

The blood drained out of Angel's face and his eyes were full of fury, but the immediate explosion was not his anger, but applause and whooping from everybody else in the room. They had just seen one hell of a hand of poker.

I stood up and bestowed them my sunniest smile, and Annabelle, letting bygones be bygones, came rushing into my arms, hugging me. Coop, smiling, was ambling up to offer his congratulations, as well.

"Now that you're a wealthy man, Bret," Annabelle said, "I feel I can find it my heart to forgive certain cruelties of yours . . ."

But someone else was less forgiving.

"You miserable cheatin' son of a bitch," the Angel was saying, and he'd pulled a revolver from a big boot, while I didn't even have a damn gun to go for.

Annabelle's scream and two nearly synchronous gunshots were a blur of simultaneous sound, but it wasn't me who'd been shot.

The Angel was about to have his only chance to live up to his name, but the odds were against him; he was headed straight down, to the floor for now, deeper down his next most likely stop, his shirt blossoming with red, his eyes wide and, for once, empty of hate. In fact, just plain empty.

The sound was like a tree falling; and Coop was standing beside me, his mouth a thin merciless line, the Colt in his right hand pointing at the target he'd just hit, its barrel twirling a lasso of gunsmoke.

But there were two Colts; we'd drawn, and fired, simultaneously, and the gun from Coop's left holster was tight in my hand.

Then, from a corner of one eye, I saw them. The sons of bitches should have beat a hasty retreat, the odds would have been better for them if they had, but no—they were as stupid as they were mean, and they came moving through the crowd with their own guns got from God-knew-where, the wandering-eyed side-winder and the rope-burned buzzard charging toward me with the murder in their hearts showing on their faces.

Coop was standing right beside me, but he didn't see them coming; his eyes were on the man he'd just shot. So I swiveled and fired and my two shots were so close together, they sounded like one.

And the two of them fell, only a fraction of a moment apart; the sidewinder's eyes had both finally stopped wandering, and the buzzard's worries about ever meeting another noose were over, forever.

Then the guns were back in Coop's holsters, him and me putting them there at the same time, as if we were of one mind and one set of instincts.

And Annabelle was back in my arms.

18

Flew the Coop

The moment had come.

The man called Marshal Zane Cooper strode to the safe that only he could open, and expertly twirled the dial. Word had spread around the ship, and people had roused themselves out of bed, filling the main salon for the final (and literal) payoff of the First Annual All-Rivers Poker Championship.

Of which I was, of course, the one and only winner.

The Commodore, hiding his frustration well, watched as Coop practically ducked inside the big safe to fetch the locked satchel of cash. When Coop turned, and stood upright, the satchel was in his left hand, and one of those pearl-handled Colts was in the other.

A collective gasp shook the room.

But Coop's solemn words were directed only to me.

"Sorry, Bret . . . I hate for you to have to end your winnin' streak like this . . ."

As he spoke he was moving toward an open window behind him, a large window that led out onto the upper-deck balcony.

I winced. "Don't do it, Coop . . ."

"I feel right poorly 'bout this, boy, but somethin' you said to me once stuck with me."

He was still backing up, the crowd held at bay by the big .45.

"You said, 'There's only one thing more important in this life than money . . . and that's more money.' "

"I didn't say that," I said, edging forward. "My pappy did."

"Stay back, boy! I don't wanna use this."

I kept edging forward. "You think you could?"

"I wouldn't kill you, I admit. But I sure as shootin' could wound you, some."

I froze.

He was half out the window when he said, "I been a lawman for a lot of years, and what do I have to show for it? Gray hair and a reputation." He shrugged. "Well, when I saw all this money, I decided I'd rather have the cash than the rep."

And he was out the window.

His footsteps echoed on the deck, as Commodore Devol yelled to the nearest bartender, "Give me a gun!

Now!" The bartender found a rifle back under behind there and handed it over. The tails of the Commodore's coat were flying as he raced after Coop. I was right behind Devol, and behind me, Annabelle was coming up fast.

Coop had taken the steps down to the lower deck, and was lowering himself into a little boat, tied up at the side. He undid the rope and the fast current began quickly carrying him downstream.

The Commodore leaned against the rail and aimed the rifle.

I grabbed it, yanked the firearm out of his hands.

He was astounded. "What the hell . . . ?"

Annabelle was beside me now; others had followed, a crowd building. A cool breeze was blowing everyone's clothing and hair—the same breeze that was aiding the man in the white Stetson who was rowing quickly away from us, a satchel full of money at his feet.

"Let him go," I said softly.

"You must be mad, son," the Commodore said.

"He saved my life," I said, and shrugged. "I only have one of those. Money, hell . . . I can always win more of that."

Annabelle was looking at me with new admiration; she clung to my arm, rested her head against my shoulder.

"Besides," I said, "I got what I came for: the championship."

The Commodore laughed hollowly, hands on his hips, as he shook his head and smiled his wonderful smile. "That's half a million dollars you just let set sail, son. Do I have to remind you of that?"

"It's *my* half a million," I said. "Do I have to remind *you* of that?"

The Commodore considered my statement.

"Look," I said. "That man probably never had a dishonest thought in his life before. And no matter what he says, he's thrown away a reputation it took a lifetime to build. He'll be haunted by this misdeed for the rest of his days."

The crowd was very quiet; it might have been a funeral.

"That's punishment enough," I said, turning away from the receding sight of the man in the rowboat. "I won't be swearing out a warrant against him."

Annabelle slipped her hand in mine.

"That's the way you want it, son?" the Commodore asked quietly.

"That's the way I want it."

He wasn't smiling, and his eyes seemed a little damp; he was visibly moved. "I know a little somethin' about money, Mr. Maverick. I made a lot of it in this lifetime, and I'll fully intend to make a whole lot more."

Now he spoke to the crowd, gathered around.

"But this young man has more wisdom about what's right and true and *really* valuable than a poor old scoundrel like me will ever have. I lost several fortunes and more than one wife because of an unnatural thirst for money, more money. Well, today—money be damned . . . and I invite all of you to join me in the main salon, where the drinks are on me! I want to raise my glass in toast to a real champion."

There was applause, amid cries of "Here! Here!", as the Commodore slipped his arm around me and walked me back inside, like a conquering hero, and kept his word.

But just one round.

In my stateroom, I helped Annabelle out of her jacket, saying, "I won't give it to you until you close your eyes."

She looked lovely in the shirt-waist blouse, though not as fetching as in the gown with its alluring bodice.

"What is it?" she asked eagerly, a happy, greedy child. "Jewelry? I do so *love* jewelry, Bret . . ."

"Close your eyes. If I tell you, it won't be a surprise."

"Oh, I just love surprises!"

So I surprised her.

I placed both hands on her shoulders, gently, then slid them down onto her full bosom. . . .

"Oh, Bret . . ."

Then I grabbed the cloth of the blouse in my fists and ripped open that lovely garment, buttons flying, cloth tearing, yanking it off entirely, as she squealed in horror, her eyes popping, hands covering her exposed self.

But it was not her creamy white skin she sought to cover, or her shapely figure, either.

She was trying, lamely, to cover a contraption worn over her slip, a ludicrously elaborate (but known to be effective) harness of pulleys, cords, and silver-plate tubing, reaching from her right forearm and disappearing down under her dress, where it would end at her knees.

To use it, she would have needed only to spread her knees slightly, in a manner that even the most delicate lady might get away with, even in mixed company, and a metal claw holding a card would slip between the layers of a double sleeve, into her palm. The Kepplinger holdout, it was called, named after its card-thief inventor, P. J. Kepplinger.

I had caught him using it once.

I let go of her.

She reddened, sitting glumly on the bed, the contraption still on her. She was embarrassed, but not because I was seeing her in her slip.

"I didn't even use the damn thing," she muttered. "Put it on after the break, and didn't even use it . . ."

"You didn't need to. You're a good player, Annabelle. You made it to the final round, and you deserved to."

"Maybe that's why I couldn't bring myself to cheat in that game. You don't suppose I'm developin' a conscience?"

"That would be a shame," I said.

"And all I would have had to do is . . ." And she held out her palm to demonstrate the device, but then her eyes went wide. "Well, imagine that!"

I sat next to her. "What?"

She showed me a crinkly chagrined grin, gestured toward the holdout contraption. "Damn thing doesn't even work. Look." She lifted her skirt to show me the cards still caught in the lower reaches of the device. "It's jammed up! It wouldn't have worked even I *had* tried it."

"Can I . . . help you off with that thing? Looks a mite uncomfortable."

"Sure . . . oh. Careful. That hurts . . . no, not that . . . yes!"

"Better get that skirt off . . ."

"That's probably wise. Oh, yes . . . that is an improvement . . . oh, Bret . . ."

When I finally tossed the thing on the floor, it belatedly lived up to its promise, as an ace of spades popped into the clawlike holder.

But neither Annabelle nor myself were much interested in cards, at that point.

The *Lauren Belle* made a firewood stop at Huggins Junction. I had no desire or need to go back to St. Louis; I could buy a horse here and head back out on the trail.

So I told Annabelle, as we walked arm-in-arm down the gangplank onto the dock.

"Where's your next stop?" I asked her.

"Somewhere's else," she said, rather sadly, I thought.

I stopped and looked at her—she sure was a lovely thing. The sun was shining bright and, from this angle, had turned the Mississippi the color of butter; but her hair was far more golden than that.

"That's a coincidence," I said.

"What is?"

"Somewhere's else is where I'm headed. Why not travel together?"

She lowered her gaze.

"After all," I said, "I could use the protection."

That made her smile, but she shook her head no. "I *want* to go with you, Bret . . . it would be wonderful, goin' with you. Such glorious arguments we could have, for so many years."

"Then why not do it, Annabelle?"

"Maybe someday, Bret darlin'. But right now . . . right now, there's somethin' I have to do, first."

"What's that?"

Her Southern accent disappeared: "I want to win a big game of my own."

She knew I understood.

We embraced; kissed. Our eyes were locked for a very long time.

Then she lowered her gaze and said, "You take care, hear?"

And she started back up the gangplank.

"Annabelle! Wait!"

She turned and winced, as if having to gaze on me again meant simply more heartbreak than she could bear.

I walked up and handed her the wallet I'd just lifted from her purse.

She smirked, but was impressed.

"Not bad," she said. "Not bad at all, for a beginner."

"Hope for me?"

She nodded, and as she put the wallet back in her purse, she removed my pocket watch from where she'd tucked it away, and pressed it into my palm.

"For both of us," she said.

And then she hurried back up the gangplank so fast, she was either truly touched by our parting, or had lifted something else.

19

Showdown

The night was as black as the inside of a clenched fist, the moon hidden behind cloud cover, no stars peeking through. The only thing throwing any light at all on this barren patch of rocks and brush was a small campfire; the only sound was that of a nearby stream, its water trickling over a rocky bed.

The tall, broad-shouldered man who stood waiting at this lonely campfire was as still as a cactus; the fire threw shadows on the crevices of his weathered, mustached face. He wore a single pearl-handled Colt .45 in a holster tied to his leg with a leather string.

Barely visible in the flicker of firelight was a satchel,

standing open, on the ground near where the man stood. Beside the satchel were two piles of money.

Two big piles.

The measured clip-clop of a horse being walked toward the camp broke the stillness.

The tall man standing by the fire drew his gun, cocked it, the sound echoing through the night.

"No need for that," a male voice said. "Let me just tie up my horse."

The tall man—Coop—holstered his pearl-handled Colt smoothly and said, "Where the hell have you been?"

Commodore Devol—who had traded in his three-piece gray suit for the crisp cowhide jacket, freshly ironed dark shirt, and stiff Levi's of the duded-up city slicker—stepped into the glow of the campfire.

"I had to say proper goodbyes to all my guests," he said. "And there was the law to deal with. Three men died on my boat, you know."

"That was your fault," Coop said tightly.

Devol bent to light his cheroot off a twig from the campfire. "You don't sound pleased to see me."

Coop stepped forward, and his voice was coldly angry. "I thought it was just you and me, in this. If you won, I'd do nothin'. If anybody else won, well . . . I'd do what I did."

"Right. What's the problem?"

"The problem is three men dead. And we're lucky it was held to that. That wasn't part of the bargain!"

The Commodore's wide smile was like a joker's. "Do you really think the world will be a lesser place, without the Angel and his trailhand trash?"

"I just don't cotton to surprises," Coop said. "Why didn't you *tell* me Angel was in on it, too?"

The Commodore shrugged. "He wasn't 'in on it'—he was just a hired hand. Besides—what was it young Maverick said to Mrs. Bransford, about never showing your hole card, till you have to?"

Coop's frown, highlighted in the fire glow, was menacing. "But what if Angel had won that game? Would we be splittin' *three* ways?"

"Of course not! He was hired help, I said. The thick-skulled bastard . . . why, he even fouled up the *real* job I gave him."

"What job?"

Devol shrugged. "I hired him to keep Maverick out of the game. I wanted to *win* that damn thing, you know. And that son-of-a-bitch is just too damn good."

Coop walked to the two piles of money. He kicked the empty satchel with the toe of a boot. "Take your money and hightail it, Devol. This concludes our partnership. I don't cotton to people who spring surprises on me."

"Well, then, you probably won't 'cotton' to this, either," the Commodore said, and when he raised his hand waist-high, a two-round derringer was in it. He cocked it back, and again the sound echoed ominously in the night.

"We had a deal," Coop said, as if it mattered.

The dazzling smile gleamed in the fire glow. "Honor among thieves? I don't think so. Maybe in a better world." The Commodore's voice dripped sarcasm as he pointed the derringer at Coop's heart. "I just want you to know what a pleasure it's been working with an *honest* man, for a change."

That was when the cocking of a third gun made its disturbing, and distinctly recognizable, echo in the night.

The cocking of my .44.

I stepped from the bushes and the shadows that had concealed me and said, "Afraid the pleasure's all mine, Commodore."

Coming up behind the Commodore, I plucked the little gun from his hand, and kept my Colt trained on Coop. I knew how fast the marshal was. Once Devol's pocket pistol was in my pocket, I slipped Coop's .45 from his holster and tossed it in the brush.

I didn't even have to tell them to put their hands up—they did it on their own, and when I gestured with my .44, they moved so they were standing next to each other nice and snug. Then I bent over the satchel and, with my left hand, placed the bundles of cash back inside.

"How'd you trail me here?" Devol demanded. "I saw you get off my ship at Huggins Junction."

"This is one time I ain't showin' my kicker," I said, grinning, "even though you *are* payin' to see it. Did you really think I was fool enough to buy that pompous speech of yours? About how wise I was, and such a real champion?"

He glowered at me, the charming smile nowhere to be seen.

I closed the satchel. Looked hard at Coop. "You, on the other hand . . . you really had me fooled, with your Western marshal bunkum. And I'm not easily suckered."

Coop's stare was hardening; it was like he was sighting a gun on me, though his hands were clearly empty.

Keeping the gun trained on both of them, I said,

"But, Marshal—you saved my life, no question. So I'm payin' you back, right now . . . by leavin' you with yours."

His voice was a low rumble. "You don't want to leave me alive, son. That would be the biggest mistake you ever made."

"You already made your big mistake, didn't you? The whole world knew what you were . . . and now the world knows what you've turned into. All your life's work, all the good you've done . . . thrown away. Blowin' in the breeze like so much sagebrush."

"You're right," Coop said, and his voice was trembling, "everything you say is the bitter truth. I traded every decent thing I ever did or had for the money in that satchel . . ."

His voice thundered through the night; I damn near dropped the pistol.

". . . so you damn well best look behind you, boy, because if you leave me here alive, I'll be comin' for you, and for *it!*"

I took a step back.

He stepped forward—even with his hands in the air, he was a threatening sight, the glow of the flames making the angles of his chiseled face starkly sinister.

"Maybe tomorrow, maybe next Christmas . . . I'll be there. Right there. Behind you. You'll drop your guard, and guess who'll be waitin'?"

I laughed. "Maybe in your prime. But now? You're just another decrepit old has-been. You couldn't sneak up on a dead man."

The Commodore got bold now, though his voice

betrayed how frayed his nerves were. "You've got the money! What more can you want? Just go—leave us!"

"I said I wasn't going to kill the marshal," I said. "I didn't say anything about lettin' *you* off for what you done."

"Maverick—" he began.

"Maybe the fairest thing to do would be let you two get back to that discussion I interrupted."

The Commodore didn't like the sound of that. "What do you mean?"

"I mean, just let one of you kill the other . . ."

And I tossed the .44 high in the air.

When I stepped back into the shadows with the satchel in hand, they were poised in wide-eyed terror, watching it come down. I should have ridden off, and I'm sure they thought I was gone, but I admit it: I'm a curious cuss.

I watched as Coop dove for the gun as it fell, and saw the Commodore trip him, but Coop was graceful for a man his size and his age, and he rolled to his feet and plucked the pistol off the dusty ground before Devol could get his hands on it.

The Commodore was on his knees and Coop was training the .44 on the pitifully begging man as I rode off into the night.

"You can run, Maverick!" Coop's voice echoed over my gelding's hoofbeats. "Run, you dog—but I'll find you! And shoot you down!"

I hadn't gone far at all when I heard the gunshots, and knew the Commodore would no longer be a problem.

20

Hole Card

There is nothing quite like the luxury of a fine hotel, and the San Franciscan was one of the finest in California. I had a deluxe suite with all the comforts home never had, but right now I was in one of the several spacious tubs of the hotel's communal bathroom, where the plush towels were as thick as the steaks in the San Franciscan Dining Room.

And if there's anything more soothing than stretching out in a hot tub with bubbles courtesy of some fancy imported bath salts, I sure couldn't tell you. My clothes were stacked near me, with my boots, and the money satchel—which I'd been taking with me everywhere these last few days—was next to me, too. As was my holstered gun.

I was half asleep and completely content.

That changed abruptly, when I heard the familiar, ominous echo of a pistol cocking, the sound bouncing off the wall tiles of the white chamber.

I hadn't even heard the door open—he was good; you had to give him that.

No need to go for my gun; he had the drop on me—standing there with his lantern jaw and his slightly beady eyes and that gray well-trimmed handle-bar mustache.

"Decrepit old has-been, is it?" Coop said.

I just watched him approach. My hand was hovering over my holstered gun.

"Couldn't sneak up on a dead man?" he snarled. "Well, I sure as hell snuck up on you, son."

I smiled, reached for the soap, and scrubbed my chest, idly. "I kind of liked that one—'sneak up on a dead man.' "

He snorted a laugh. "Lucky for you I have such a Christian and forgiving nature."

"I trust the Commodore will not be a problem."

He sat on the edge of the tub opposite me and smiled sunnily. "Not after I fired those blanks at him, from that gun you tossed me." He lowered his voice and approximated rage. " 'I never did commit a cold-blooded murder in my long career, but I plan to make two exceptions—the next time I see Maverick, and the next time I see you!' "

I laughed, and so did he; it echoed pleasantly in the room.

"That's what the buzzard gets," I said, "for cheating Bart on the *Lauren Belle*."

He nodded firmly. "Worth all the time and trouble, nailing that crooked bastard's hide to the wall."

"As my ole pappy used to say, 'Cheating a cheater is a deeply rewarding, even religious experience.'"

Figured out my hole card yet? Have a look.

"I don't remember saying any such thing," Pappy said, "and furthermore, I don't appreciate you referring to me as 'old,' all the time. Your mother and I had you boys at a tender age."

"Yes, we were both very young at birth, I understand."

He frowned, as he dug a cheroot out of his jacket and lighted it up. "That's not my meaning, and you know it. You've been misquoting me all your young life, and I'm plumb tired of it—"

"If I quoted you accurately, the dumb things you *do* come up with, how would that sound? I've got to improve on 'em."

He was about to reply, then he scratched his head. "You know, son, I haven't checked in just yet, but that bath looks mighty inviting. . . . Think the hotel would mind?"

"Pull up a tub, Pappy."

Before long Pappy was in the tub across from me, enjoying the hot water and bubbly bath salts, showing me a few tricks with a deck of cards. Nobody could do the Maverick shuffle better than Pappy himself.

"Poor illiterate fools," he said, "thinking a dime novel character was a real man."

"Lot of people read Ned Buntline's tales about 'Mar-

shal Zane Cooper,' Pappy—and it says 'true' story on
the front of 'em."

"The best way to sell a lie is to label it the truth,
son."

I'd have to remember that one.

"You know, Bret," he said, "I about had a conniption
fit when you let that feller Angel cut the cards, after I
went to all that trouble to put that ace of spades on top
of the deck for you."

"Maybe I'm capable of conjuring up an ace without
your help," I said. "Maybe I'm blessed with magic, or
just plain luck."

"Or maybe after he cut 'em, you just put the deck
back the way I had it."

I was smoking a cheroot, too. I blew a smoke ring,
and grinned. "Maybe."

The *click* of the cocking pistol made its familiar, ever
ominous echo.

Neither one of us turned; we didn't have to. We
hadn't even heard the door open. She was good—you
had to give her that much.

Without so much as a greeting, Annabelle—in her
money-green traveling costume—was training her little
pistol on us with one hand, and moving our clothes,
boots and guns away from our tubs, with the other.

Then she filled her pretty hand with the handle of
the satchel.

"You'll find a lovely gift waitin' at the front desk,
Bret," she said sweetly, Southern accent in full
blossom.

"And what would that be?"

"A brand-new silk shirt . . . imported from Paris, France. To make up for the one I ruined."

Pappy seemed genuinely touched. "Why, that's sweet, Annabelle. That's right sweet."

"Hey," I said, "don't be so amiable. She's *robbing* us."

"What's your real name?" she asked him. "I'm not about to call you 'Pappy.' "

"Even should you ever have the misfortune to marry this rapscallion," Pappy said, "I would appreciate it if you did not 'honor' me with that appellation. It's Beauregard, my dear . . . but close friends call me 'Beau.' "

She smiled one-sidedly and shook her head; the ribboned-back blond curls shimmered. "You *are* a remarkable family," she admitted.

"How did you figure it out?" I asked her.

She smirked. "Give me *some* credit, please! You have a few 'tells,' yourselves. You're both the same height, the same build, you have the same beady eyes—"

Pappy sat up in his bubble bath. "I object to that characterization!"

". . . you both kiss the same . . ."

"What did you say?" I sputtered.

". . . you both draw your guns the same way, and you both sing the same *wrong* words to 'Amazing Grace.' It's 'blind but now I'm free,' not 'bound,' you dumb jackasses."

Pappy had a puzzled expression. "You certain of that, m'dear?"

"Dead certain." She peeked first in his tub, then mine. "And, of course, there are certain other physical

characteristics you have in common . . . but why don't
we just leave it at that?"

And, our satchel in her pretty little hand, she blew
us a kiss—whether meant for Pappy, or me, or both of
us, I couldn't say, though I would imagine Pappy and I
might have differing opinions on the subject—and she
did, in fact, leave it at that.

The click of the door closing was far less ominous
than all these damn guns cocking.

Pappy leaned back in his tub and drew on his
cheroot.

"You don't seem terribly upset, Pappy."

"Good-looking woman like that won't be hard to
track. Wonder which of us she trailed here?"

I shrugged. "Who knows? That was her hole card,
and she didn't show us."

Pappy was smiling, lost in a kind of reverie. "You
know, son—if someone had to rob us, I'm glad it was
my little Annie."

I sat up and water splashed out of the tub.

"Your little *who*? Your little *what*? Don't you think
you're a mite old for a gal that age?"

"She's a woman, son."

"Well, the thought of you and her, and I say this
keeping in mind you're the man who raised me, and
that I hold you in the highest regard, of course . . ."

"Of course."

"It's disgusting."

He chuckled. "My, my . . . son, didn't I ever tell
you that envy is the one shade of green that ain't
worth cultivatin'?"

"Oh, you're right, I'm jealous," I said, actually a

little irritated now. "What's a minor age difference, anyway? After all, when she's a hundred, you'll only be a hundred-thirty-five."

He waggled two cheroot-bearing fingers at me, lecture-style. "I would be careful in choosing my words, were I you, son. That splendid creature may one day be your stepmother."

"She was a hell of a lot closer to being *your* daughter-in-law!"

"Now," he said, "that would have been a sheer disaster—you're lacking in the maturity, the experience, required to satisfy the needs of a woman like Annabelle."

"That's not what she said to me."

"All I know," he said, as if he were sad, "is what *she* told me, in confidence, about *you*, and certain . . . deficiencies of yours in, shall we say, the romantic arena?"

"You're lyin' through your teeth."

He shrugged. "I might be."

Then we started to laugh; it made a pleasant echo in the tiled room.

"So," Pappy said, "what we wind up with for all our efforts is a one-half-million-dollar imported silk shirt."

"No," I said, thinking about it. "It's more like one half-million dollars *and* an imported silk shirt . . . that satchel's full of cut-up seed catalog pages."

A touch Annabelle would appreciate.

Pappy's eyes were bright, and his smile was pure greed. "Well, hell's bell's, son—where's the money, then?"

"In my boots. Your half's in the left one."

I got out of the tub and went dripping over to where Annabelle had moved our things, got the boot with Pappy's share, and handed it to him.

His smile eased into something wonderful, something proud, as he took the bundled bills from their leather home.

And I must admit I felt proud, too, pleased with what my pappy and I had accomplished. He was clearly looking for the right words to express this tender sentiment, but for once, words seemed to be failing him.

As he sat there in the tub, riffling through the greenbacks, he said, fondly, "Bret . . . son . . . there's something I have to tell you."

"What, Pappy?"

"Feels like you shorted me. This thing ain't well and truly settled till we can get back to the room and count it."

"That could take all week," I said testily, "with your fingers-and-toes arithmetic."

He was considering a comeback, but then he gave me the sunny smile instead, and stuffed the bills back in the boot. Since I was still out of the tub, I put a chair under the door knob, at an angle, in case Annabelle came back.

Then I returned to my warm soapy bath and Pappy and I relaxed there, together. A quiet family moment.

I began to hum "Amazing Grace," and after while, Pappy joined in on the harmony. Perfect and rich and full, it sounded, reverberating in the tiled chamber like a full choir.

And we sang the words any damn way we pleased.

A Tip of the Stetson

In addition to acknowledging William Goldman for his wry, lively screenplay, I would like to express my gratitude to Roy Huggins, creator of the original television series, and, of course, James Garner. Their inspiration made this a fun project for a childhood fan of this classic show.

Poker According to Maverick (Dell, 1959) by Bret himself (his likely ghost writer being his creator) was an essential source for Bret and his pappy's outlook on the games of poker and life. The young-adult novel, *Maverick* by Charles I. Coombs (Whitman, 1959), indicated how another writer had skillfully solved many of the problems I would face.

This novel intends to invoke not the real West, but the mythic one, specifically as described in *Warner Bros. Television* by Lynn Wooley, Robert W. Malsbary, and Robert G. Strange, Jr. (McFarland, 1985). Nonetheless, several nonfiction works were also useful, including the Time-Life Books *Old West* series, volumes: *The Rivermen* (1975) and *The Gamblers* (1978); *The Look of the West* by Foster-Harris (Bonanza Books, 1960); and *The Writer's Guide to Everyday Life in the 1800s* by Marc McCutcheon (Writer's Digest Books, 1993). I would also like to thank western writer W. W. Lee for her generous advice and impromptu research help.

Finally, thanks to my agent Dominick Abel, Sue Berger of Penguin UK, and Grace Ressler of Warner Bros. for giving me the opportunity, and providing the support.

Published or forthcoming

SLIVER

Ira Levin
author of *Rosemary's Baby*

Thirteen hundred Madison Avenue, an elegant 'sliver' building, soars high and narrow over Manhattan's smart Upper East Side. Kay Norris, a successful single woman, moves on to the twentieth floor of the building, high on hopes of a fresh start and the glorious Indian summer outside. But she doesn't know that someone is listening to her. Someone is *watching* her.

'Levin really knows how to touch the nerve ends' – *Evening Standard*

'*Sliver* is the ultimate *fin de siècle* horror novel, a fiendish goodbye-wave to trendy urban living … Ira Levin has created the apartment dweller's worst nightmare' – Stephen King

SIGNET

Published or forthcoming

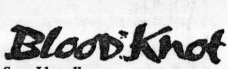

Sam Llewellyn

Bill Tyrrell has locked the door on his crusading past. As a reporter, he's seen conflict and pain close up – and not once have his words ever saved a life. Now he's back in England, living on the antique cutter *Vixen*, the only legacy from his long-vanished father. But the journalist in him can't be buried. Not when a Russian sea cadet gets wrapped round the *Vixen's* propeller under the eyes of a Cabinet Minister – and Tyrrell becomes the scapegoat . . .

It is the first in a series of harrowing accidents. And suddenly the past begins to open up all over again, as Tyrrell's battle-hardened reporting reflexes lure him into a dark maze of political cover-ups and violent death . . .

'The best seaborne thriller in many a tide'
– *Daily Mail*